12-METRE IMAGES

12-METRE IMAGES

Bob Fisher

PELHAM BOOKS
London

For Noel Robins, Challenging Skipper and Executive Director of the Royal Perth Yacht Club's Defence of the America's Cup; a world champion yachtsman with the difficulties of guiding the America's Cup through the new commercial demands – a present.

First published in Great Britain by
Pelham Books Ltd
27 Wrights Lane
Kensington
London W8 5DZ
1986

British Library Cataloguing in Publication Data

Fisher, Bob
    12-metre images.
    1. Yacht racing—History
    I. Title
    797.1′4   GV826.5

ISBN 0 7207 1713 2

Typeset in 14/16 pt Optima Roman by
Wilmaset, Birkenhead, Wirral, Great Britain
Printed in Singapore by Tien Wah Press PTE Limited

Endpapers
Southern Cross in Newport's evening sun.

Half-title
America II (US 42) smashing into the Fremantle chop.

Title page
1979 World Championship. *Windrose* (ex-*Chanceggar*) chases the 1958 America's Cup winner *Columbia*.

CONTENTS

ACKNOWLEDGEMENTS

In satisfying my addiction to 12-Metres, I am eternally grateful to the newspapers and magazines who have commissioned me to write about them. Particularly I would like to thank *The Guardian* and *The Observer* for sending me to Newport during the Cup summers, which allowed me to spend rather more time there than otherwise. And to *Yachts & Yachting* and *Boat International* from whom I have lifted some of the material I wrote for them for this book.

I would also like to thank Peter de Savary for many things. Firstly for mounting a challenge that went a long way to making Britain a 12-Metre force and secondly for his generous hospitality. There may never be another challenge quite like that of the *Victory* Syndicate but many will reflect its drive and purpose.

It is difficult to acknowledge the assistance of something that no longer exists but I must try. Southern Television, in promoting the 1979 world championship, helped to engender interest in the class in Britain. From that the *Lionheart* challenge for the America's Cup benefited and out of that came the 1983 *Victory* effort which in turn provided the impetus to the Royal Thames YC challenge for the America's Cup in 1987. While Southern Television lost their franchise in Britain, their efforts in the 12-Metre world do not go unrewarded.

Many are the people who have helped in the preparation of this book, most notably among them John Oakeley, Ed Dubois and Ian Howlett. I hope they may enjoy it. In addition I would like to thank all those 12-Metre sailors who have taken time out to talk to me about their boats over the years and most especially to those who have invited me to sail with them. There isn't anything quite like 12-Metre racing.

I would also like to acknowledge the assistance of the International Yacht Racing Union for allowing me to reproduce part of the 12-Metre Rating Rule.

The book would never have happened without Lesley Gowers, the editor at Pelham Books who knew exactly how to prod me and how to let me have free rein when things were difficult.

Bob Fisher
Lymington
April 1986

1 AN INTRODUCTION TO 12-METRES

The America's Cup, 134 ounces of sterling silver, crafted by Robert Garrard in 1848, won by the schooner *America* for a race around the Isle of Wight in 1851, and appropriately bottomless in view of the amount of money spent on twenty-six challenges and defence campaigns.

Left
Sverige and *Lionheart* racing in Marstrand Fiord after *Lionheart* had completed a four-day sea passage to sail against her Swedish opponent.

The 12-Metre Class would have died but for the America's Cup. In the early 1950s it was all but moribund; the huge economic change wrought by a global conflict had seen the bigger boats wiped from the face of yachting and the 'Twelves' were part of that dying era. The few that were left had mostly been converted for cruising, with engines fitted, and even their smaller sisters, the 'Sixes', were heading for permanent retirement.

Only a small group of sailors on both sides of the Atlantic, pressuring for a change in the Deed of Gift of the America's Cup, gave lifeblood to the 12-Metre Class. The behemoths of the J-class would never again grace Newport Sound; zillionaires were not in evidence, and the most exotic craft within reasonable (sic) financial limits would be those of around 45-foot waterline length, a restriction which fitted the 12-Metres. The Deed of Gift was changed on 17 December 1956 and 12-Metres began a new and rarified existence, but even as Commodore Elbridge T. Gerry and Secretary John H. Bird of the New York Yacht Club, put their signatures to the amendment of the deed made ninety-nine years earlier, they cannot have foreseen what was to happen three decades on. For the growth of the 12-Metre Class was not to take place for very many years and probably would not have done so at all had not some of the sailors decided that there was more to racing the boats than the America's Cup. They were once-every-three-years racing craft and as such dreadfully certain to be responsible for their own genocide.

The change came with multiple challenges, first instituted in 1970; unbeknown to the New York Yacht Club these were to sound the death knell of its

1

tenure of the Holy Grail of yachting. Until that time the only other racing for the 12-Metre Class, the New York Yacht Club Cruise aside, was in the Defender Selection Trials, the reason for American superiority. More than one challenger – and in 1970 there were *Gretel II* and *France 1* – meant that the challengers had competitive racing rather than simply working out against their trial horses, and competitive racing meant a dramatic improvement in performance.

Newport, Rhode Island, thus remained the epicentre of 12-Metre activity, and it was not until John Oakeley, the 1980 British America's Cup challenging skipper, sought competition for *Lionheart* prior to shipping to the United States that anyone

The mast comes down on *Sverige* for the second time in the 1979 World Championship at Brighton. At the time she was neck and neck with *Lionheart* in the deciding race.

Pelle Petterson, World Champion in both Stars and 6-Metres. An outstanding sailor who promoted the first Swedish challenge, designed the yacht and skippered her.

Overleaf
Windrose, formerly *Chanceggar*, chases *Columbia* during the '79 World Championship. *Windrose* was bought by a Dutch syndicate, ever hopeful of raising an America's Cup challenge; *Columbia*, the 1958 defender, has now been converted for cruising.

actively tried to race the existing 12-Metres. Oakeley believed that if the cup were to change hands, there had to be co-operation between the challengers, and he found that Sweden's Pelle Petterson, who challenged for the cup in 1977, was of like mind. Between them they arranged for a series of seven races to be held at Marstrand in Sweden and the impecunious British syndicate made the decision to sail *Lionheart* there on her own bottom – shades of the early America's Cups when the challengers had to journey across the Atlantic in the same way. The series was a huge success, enjoyed by all who took part, and resulted in a narrow win for *Lionheart*.

Oakeley had felt duty bound to offer Petterson similar hospitality with a series in Britain. He had the support of his club, the nominated challengers for 1980, the Royal Southern Yacht Club and, in turn, the sponsorship of Southern Television, then one of the contracting companies in Britain's independent commercial network. Together they organised the first-ever World Championship of the 12-Metre Class, at Brighton at the end of the summer of 1979. It began with two days of fleet racing and progressed, naturally, to a round-robin match racing series. There were six entries from four countries: Sweden, Holland and Australia as well as Britain were represented. There might even have been an entry from the United States but for the veto of the New York Yacht Club's America's Cup Committee.

American Russell Long had agreed to ship *Clipper* to the championship; the author of this book represented Southern Television in the negotiations which were held over lunch in the West 44th Street Manhattan clubhouse of the NYYC. Long was keen to compete; he too felt that racing these craft was the best way to improve the standards of technique; but the attitude of the club was against him. He was warned that if he took part he would not be considered as a defence candidate in 1980! The NYYC held the ultimate authority as to what could, or could not, be done with any American 12-Metre as long as it held the America's Cup.

3

Nonetheless the first World Championship was a total success, even if some of the competitors were past their prime. *Columbia* and *Constellation* had defended the cup for America and *Gretel II* had been the challenger in 1970. *Windrose*, the first Dutch 12-Metre for fifty years, was formerly known as the French *Chanceggar*. *Lionheart* won the championship when *Sverige*'s mast toppled, for the second time, in the final race. Petterson collected up the pieces and returned to Sweden a wiser man.

As a direct result of that racing Oakeley knew that *Lionheart* lacked speed and determined to go ahead with the most radical development seen in the class since Olin Stephens parted the rudder from the keel when he designed *Intrepid* in 1967. Oakeley and Ian Howlett, who was then working for the former's design company, had found a way to increase the area of the mainsail within the class rules. They designed a mast with a very flexible top. This was induced to bend in a deep curve above the hounds and, without limiting cross-widths, the mainsail was increased in area by more than 100 square feet. The performance improvement was well in excess of expectation. Developments above the waterline are usually more difficult to keep secret, but in this case it was not until *Lionheart* appeared in Newport that anyone took notice.

It was then that Ben Lexcen saw the way to improve *Australia*. His was a last-minute effort with the three-year-old boat, and had he started his mast design three weeks earlier cup history might have been changed sooner. The Australians never did succeed in making the big sail rig work in more than moderate winds, but in the light airs Australia did take one race from the American *Freedom* and was far ahead in another which was abandoned when the time limit ran out. The International Yacht Racing Union effectively banned the 'bendy' mast as an unsuitable development two months later when it restricted the cross-widths of the mainsail in the class.

Above
Australia II and *Victory '83* in among the spectator craft for the pre-start manoeuvres during the Challenger Selection Finals in 1983. This has been referred to as 'the mating dance of the lead-bottomed dollar-gobblers'.

Below
Dennis Conner speed-testing sails off Newport aboard *Magic*. Conner steers while Chrissie Steinman operates the stadimeter and Tom Whidden takes note of the details.

6

America's Dennis Conner had rewritten the text-book for success in the 12-Metre Class with his campaign for 1980. He sailed 300 days a year for three years preparing *Freedom* with *Enterprise*. His determination, discipline and logical development, coupled with his undoubted talent, made him almost unbeatable. Yet his Achilles' heel lay in his logicality, for it left little room for radical design. In his 1983 campaign, however, Conner sought to overcome that weakness and had two very different boats, from opposite ends of the displacement scale: *Magic* and *Spirit of America*, the one the smallest 12-Metre ever built and the other a big boat by contemporary standards. Conner launched his new boats early and the rest of the world had to follow suit, causing a period of introspection to fall upon the 12-Metre Class.

A shortage of good-quality masts for the *Victory* squad in Nassau meant a constant repair programme. Each time a mast had to come out and a new one go in to one of the Twelves, it was known as a 'Royal Tournament'.

Dennis Conner, the man who changed the face of the America's Cup by sailing 12-Metres almost every day for three years to prepare himself and his crew for the 1980 defence. Generally acknowledged as the world's finest match-racing skipper, Conner can only be held guilty of one major mistake – in the final race for the cup in 1983.

Australia II met fellow Australian *Challenge 12* in Melbourne while the other Australian challenger *Advance* met *Gretel II* in Sydney; the Italians, new to the game, and the French, by now old hands, hid themselves away to do their own thing; the Canadians were forced to do the same because of the lack of playmates in their area. The British, however, felt that they had a great deal to learn and set about it with a fanfare of trumpets. Peter de Savary wanted the world to know what his 12-Metre effort was all about and, having bought *Australia* from Alan Bond as the previous cup races ended, used her to race with the Ed Dubois-designed *Victory* and, later, *Lionheart*.

There was one attempt to bring the Twelves together: at the end of summer 1982 with the Xerox World Cup in Newport, Rhode Island. Once again the New York Yacht Club put a veto on its yachts taking part and even refused Star Class world champion, Tom Blackaller, permission to charter *Intrepid* from the Canadians for the event. It was a series which had its moments, the worst being when de Savary, at the wheel of *Australia II* on port tack, T-boned *France 3*. The best was when *Lionheart*, with no restriction of having to tack unnecessarily, won a race around Conanicut Island, going away: she was always known to be fast in a straight line but slow in manoeuvring. *Victory* won the cup and hardly ever sailed again. She was sent for hull modifications and a new keel, but when she was ready her successor, *Victory '83*, had been launched and the internal politics of the *Victory* squad kept the unsuitable *Lionheart* in commission at the expense of the much-altered *Victory*. No one will ever know if the modified Dubois design was faster than the Howlett-designed *Victory '83*.

Perhaps the highlight of the *Victory* campaign came with the two 12-Metres *Australia* and *Lionheart* being shipped to Nassau for the winter. There were certain budgetary limitations to this winter operation, as the shoreside crew were to discover. Masts were in short supply and the boisterous seas off

Providence Island would have been better preparation for Fremantle than Newport. Masts therefore suffered frequent damage and usually needed overnight repair. The process of lifting them out of the boats, performing such renovations as were possible during the night and restepping the spar in the boat for the next morning's sailing was known by the operations manager, 'Spud' Spedding, as a 'Royal Tournament'.

Perhaps de Savary's biggest scoop concerned a 12-Metre mast. A long-needed new one arrived in Nassau aboard HMS *Hermes* (one of whose crew members happened to be Prince Andrew). It was then taken the wrong way down a one-way street – Nassau's Front Street to be precise – by the entire *Victory* squad, much to the consternation of the local traffic and public at large.

A new mast for the *Victory* squad, delivered to Nassau on board HMS *Hermes*, being taken the wrong way down Nassau's Front Street. Operations manager, 'Spud' Spedding, gives hands-off encouragement.

The summer of 1983 was a much too serious time for enjoyment of 12-Metre fleet racing, but there was more match racing, for the Louis Vuitton Cup, than there had ever before been in a cup summer. The challenger selections with their three round robins, semi-finals and finals needed 153 match races and there can be no doubt that these were a huge contributory factor to the America's Cup being won by *Australia II*. John Bertrand and his crew were honed to a fine competitive edge by almost daily racing. The lesson is there for 1987 with twice the number of challengers than there were in Newport and a dilution of talent among the Australian campaigns. But it has been argued that the vast number of races which will be needed this time to determine the winner of the Louis Vuitton Cup may result in the finalists only meeting three times before their sail-off to challenge for the cup and that may be counter-productive to the exercise. On the other hand, there will be a greater degree of expertise in Fremantle than was ever assembled in Newport.

2 WHAT IS A 12-METRE?

The obvious misconception about 12-Metres is that they are 12 metres long – far from it. They vary in length, from about 62 feet overall to 70 feet, but even that is not one of the measures of the boat. Twelve metres is the rating of the craft based on an international formula dating back to 1906:

$$R = \frac{L + 2d - F + \sqrt{S}}{2.37}$$

Where:
L = length in metres
d = girth difference in metres
F = freeboard in metres
S = sail area in square metres

This, of course, is an oversimplification. 'L', for example, is not the overall length of the boat nor the waterline length; it is the 'correct length' and to find it needs some crafty measurement involving percentages of the class rating above the waterline. The 'correct length' therefore does take into consideration the sailing length of the boat when heeled, and since hollows are not allowed in the surface of the hull above the waterline, the formula is substantially accurate in assessing the true waterline of the boat.

The girth difference is a means of assessing the displacement of the yacht as a factor affecting the rating and is described in the International Yacht Racing Union rule of the 12-Metre Class in the following manner: 'The girth difference, "d" in the formula, shall be measured in a transverse plane, vertically, at 0.55 L.W.L. (0.55 girth station) and shall be the sum of the differences between the skin girth and chain girth, measured on the two sides of the yacht, from a mark on the covering board to

The profile of *Victory '83*, now in Italian hands, showing the relationship of genoa to mainsail. The principal strain areas in the sails are in Kevlar cloth, the rest in Dacron, both supporting a Mylar film.

corresponding points in the hull surface at a level 12.5 per cent of the class rating (1500 mm) below the waterline.' There is also a formula which relates displacement (by weighing the boat) to the waterline length. If a yacht is less than the displacement required by the rule for her waterline length, a penalty is added to the 'L' measurement based on the difference of what it is and what it should be.

The freeboard ('F') is the sum of three freeboards, one near the bow, one near the stern and one at the readily used 0.55 girth station. There are inter-related limits to the individual components. A penalty is applied if the freeboard is too low.

Right
New Zealand 5, with her sister ship, *New Zealand 3*, were the first two glass-fibre 12-Metres ever built. The Kiwis argued that their technology in using this material would give them an edge and they spent several months convincing Lloyds of London that they could build a 12-Metre of similar characteristics to ones constructed in aluminium.

Lionheart hangs in her sling at the Newport Shipyard. Designed by Ian Howlett, *Lionheart* is a good example of a heavy displacement 12-Metre.

The first aluminium-built 12-Metre ever was Alan Bond's *Southern Cross*. The holes cut in her after-deck, which are not allowed under the current Rule, were not simply to lighten the boat but to encourage a free-flow of air to cool the under-deck area in the middle of the boat where the winch-grinders worked (under the Rule they now have to work on deck or in 'pits').

The sail area ('S') is obtained by adding the rated area of the mainsail to the rated area of the foretriangle. The mainsail area is calculated by a simple length of hoist multiplied by the length of the foot divided by two. There are, however, limits to the height of the mast – the head of the mainsail must not be hoisted more than 25.18 metres above the height of the covering board abreast of the mast. The limit of the foretriangle is 18.93 metres. The rated area of the foretriangle is 85 per cent of the base of it multiplied by half the vertical height, and only sails with a maximum foot length of less than the base of the foretriangle plus 4.8 metres may be set in it. Extra limitations to the cross-widths of the mainsail and the length of the battens further restrict the sail makers and designers and there are also limits to the size of spinnakers.

Victory, the first of the new boats for Peter de Savary's syndicate, designed by Ed Dubois, shows a typical 12-Metre underbody. She underwent minor alterations but was never seriously raced against her Howlett-designed stablemate, *Victory '83*.

There are other limitations too, all fine tuning of an eighty-year-old rule. The scantlings of the 12-Metre Class are carefully controlled by Lloyd's of London and they have approved the building of 12-Metres in wood, aluminium (first boat, *Southern Cross*, in 1973) and composite glassfibre construction (first boat, *New Zealand 3*, in 1985). The Lloyd's scantlings endeavour to produce yachts which are as near equal in strength and weight whatever construction is used. Aluminium found quick favour because it was a cheaper building material than wood and its strength characteristics made stiffer boats. The first two glassfibre craft hit the water at the end of 1985 and their progress will be carefully monitored before others follow the New Zealand lead.

Measurement points on 12-Metres are recorded on the boats, the upside-down triangle on the waterline at the 0.55 girth station being most obvious when the boats are sailing.

3 IN THE BEGINNING

Britain's John Illingworth, the founder of the Sydney-Hobart race, was one of the early protagonists to revive the America's Cup after the Second World War. He had discussions with De Courcey Fales in 1946 and 1948, when Fales was commodore of the New York Yacht Club, but it was not until another decade had passed that the rules were changed to allow the competition to take place in 12-Metres, a class in which no boats had been built since 1939.

The Americans started with a huge advantage. In 1939 Olin Stephens had designed *Vim* which was shipped to Britain for the season and recorded nineteen firsts, four seconds and two thirds in twenty-seven starts. *Vim* was so superior to all the boats she met that she caused considerable embarrassment. She was, however, no embarrassment for the New York Yacht Club when trials to select a defender for the America's Cup began in 1958, except perhaps that, in the hands of 'Bus' Mosbacher, she looked capable of winning against the three new Twelves.

Vim was to the Americans what no other boat could possibly be for any challenger for the America's Cup: the very best benchmark in the world. After watching some of the early American trials, Illingworth was moved to write, 'It was clear that the old-timer was going to give the new yachts something to think about.' Characteristically, he was correct. The only way the NYYC Selection Committee was able to satisfy itself as to who should be the defender against Britain's *Sceptre* was to hold a special three-race series after the final trials in which *Vim* would meet *Columbia*, Stephens's latest 12-Metre. The series went all the way and *Columbia* only clinched the right to be the seventeenth

Left
A spinnaker about to be hoisted on *Gretel II*.

Overleaf
Gretel II, even in the later days of her long racing career, was a powerful performer in light airs.

defender with a twelve-second win in the third race. The summer scoreline makes interesting reading. Out of all the times they met, *Vim* beat *Columbia* by a margin of ten races to nine, but in the official trials the score was 7–5 in *Columbia*'s favour.

Columbia's win in the cup races at the expense of *Sceptre* is well chronicled. It was highly embarrassing for the British challenger. *Columbia*'s life afterwards was also full; she was immediately back in action as one of the trialists for the next challenge, only to be defeated by a rebuilt *Weatherly* of the same vintage. *Vim* had gone to Australia and become the benchmark for *Gretel*, which is perhaps why the first Australian challenge was so good and why the Australians persisted with their quest. *Vim* later became converted for cruising, as also did *Columbia* after several years in the hands of Baron Bich and another French syndicate, and a short spell on charter to Britain for the 1979 World Championship.

The importance of a good trial horse is often misunderstood; the absence of one, until very recently, amounted to a total lack of performance knowledge. Only the development of reliable micro-electronic recording equipment can give the crew of a 12-Metre any true idea of her performance and then that must be compared with data recorded earlier from another boat. *Sceptre* had only an old boat to test herself against; *Gretel*, on the other hand, had *Vim* and, when she began her work-up against the American 12-Metre, it became clear gradually that Alan Payne's creation had it in her to beat the old lady. That in itself meant that *Gretel* would go to Newport with her crew knowing that they were possibly in the same league as the Americans. When they won a race it was therefore not surprising, but even that win stretched the long arm of coincidence. It happened on 18 September 1962, twenty-eight years to the day that the defender of the cup had last lost a race: when Sir T.O.M. Sopwith's *Endeavour* beat Harold Vanderbilt's *Rainbow* by fifty-one seconds. *Gretel*'s forty-seven-second win set Newport alight and the revelry of the Australian contingent in town was not muted until the early hours – it was as well for *Gretel* supporters that skipper Jock Sturrock had asked for a lay-day after the race, even if his decision was to backfire on him when the weather changed from the fresh breeze the Australian boat and crew liked to a typical Newport Sound light-air day.

The lack of a capable trial horse was to show when Britain challenged for the cup again in 1964. To compound the felony even more, the two British syndicates built identical boats and had no idea how slow they were until they met the defender, *Constellation*, in the cup races. They must have had their suspicions but that did not deter them from making

Sparkman & Stephens designed *Columbia* to be the first 12-Metre defender of the America's Cup. She took some time to show superiority to her twenty-year-old sister, *Vim*, but defeated the British *Sceptre* more than easily.

Baron Bich's *France* culminated a design programme completed by André Mauric. Here the Goodyear blimp keeps an eye on her during her races against *Southern Cross*, perhaps a good idea because of the Baron's known propensity for getting lost in the fog.

the weakest challenge in the history of the America's Cup with *Constellation* winning one of the races by twenty minutes! How the Americans laughed at the naivety of the British.

One might be forgiven for believing that the Australians knew the match-winning plan, but before their second challenge in 1967 Sir Frank Packer altered *Gretel* underwater so that the new 12-Metre, *Dame Pattie*, had no data base against which to compare her performance assessments. The problem was further clouded by the old newspaper magnate's insistence that *Gretel* should be considered a challenger. Packer lost out – Sturrock had had enough of him and skippered *Dame Pattie*, taking key members of the crew with him – and Australia's challenge failed.

In the United States, Bill Strawbridge fronted a syndicate which built *Intrepid* and one of his first moves was to charter the 1964 winner and put her in racing trim as a trial horse. This was particularly important as Olin Stephens was intending to depart from the accepted 12-Metre design philosophy quite radically. With *Constellation* as a benchmark, Stephens would soon know if his tank-testing figures were anything like accurate. The 'Master from Madison Avenue' had decided that *Intrepid* should have a rudder separate from the keel and had tested seven different designs in the tank.

The idea was not new (is anything ever in yachting?); the practice had already been used by Stephens (and others) for offshore racers. Dick Carter had used it for his Fastnet Race winner *Rabbit*, and it was to him that Olin Stephens turned for consultation. Over $30,000, an unheard-of sum in those days, was spent on tank testing before Stephens was satisfied, and when *Intrepid* was built he was not surprised when she was able to beat *Constellation* consistently.

Intrepid marked the beginning of a new era of 12-Metres and her 4–0 win over *Dame Pattie* with margins varying between three and a half and six minutes adequately displayed her superiority. The

In 1964 *Constellation*, here seen ahead of *Columbia*, took a while to establish her place to defend the America's Cup by beating *American Eagle* and went on to record the biggest-ever winning margin over *Sovereign*.

attention that Stephens had applied to detail had added to his world beater and it was this detail which Alan Payne was not slow to notice when he was commissioned to design *Gretel II* for the third Australian challenge.

Intrepid had her winch mechanisms below the deck where three or four men worked constantly. They never saw the racing: they were the 'men-motors' to provide the power for the sail trimmers, and they were there because it reduced windage and put the weight down lower. Having taken the 'coffee grinders' off the deck, Stephens was then able to design a rig with a lower-than-normal boom. Experiments which he had commissioned Halsey Herreshoff to examine at Massachusetts Institute of Technology displayed a considerable improvement in the efficiency of the mainsail when the boom was lowered, due to the 'end plate' effect of the deck. It was the equivalent of a 'barrier fence' on the wing of an aircraft. Stephens also consulted the crew members of *Intrepid* about the layout of the gear and their input was another important facet in the production of a race-winning boat.

The testing tanks hold a fascination for Stephens. He had first resorted to them in 1936 when involved with Starling Burgess on the design of the J-class *Ranger*, and he returned there to design the successor to *Intrepid*, only to learn that tanks are far from infallible as a means of testing. Their data has to be viewed with circumspection. 12-Metres with long waterlines, and therefore heavy displacement, provide good figures from the models in the tanks, but they lack the acceleration so essential for match racing. Winning the America's Cup is what 12-Metre design is all about and it is a match-racing event where acceleration means more than sheer speed. Stephens lost sight of this when he designed *Valiant* from the figures he received from Pete de Saix of the Steven's Institute at Hoboken, New Jersey. De Saix, incidentally, was brought out of retirement to tank test the designs of the Heart of America syndicate's designs for the Chicago Yacht Club 1987 challenge.

A sight which would never be possible in the America's Cup – *Columbia* to windward of *Windrose* (ex *Chanceggar*) in the World Championship at Brighton in 1979. *Chanceggar* was a non-qualifier for the America's Cup by virtue of being American-designed and Swiss-built for a French owner.

Valiant turned out to be nearly the biggest 12-Metre ever built. She had a displacement of 69,000 lbs – only Charley Morgan's *Heritage* was bigger at 70,500 lbs on a 50-foot waterline. *Valiant* also turned out to be the only 12-Metre failure to come out of the Sparkman & Stephens offices.

For the twenty-first defence of the America's Cup, Bill Strawbridge approached Britton Chance to re-design *Intrepid*. 'Britty' had had a spectacular career as a naval architect, alternating between triumph and disaster and described by cup buff Norris Hoyt as 'tactless as he is talented, impatient as he is brilliant, and as well-connected as a computer'. Chance had worked with de Saix in the tanks as a teenager and in the design offices of Ray Hunt and Ted Hood before starting out on his own. Much of his work was in the 5.5-Metre Class where boats of his design won every World Championship between 1967 and 1972 and the gold medal at the 1968 Olympics. Chance was given the opportunity to design a 12-Metre by Baron Bich: *Chanceggar*, named after the designer and builder, Herman Eggar. It was a stepping stone for the Strawbridge alterations.

Debate has always been heated as to whether Chance's alterations to *Intrepid* made her faster or slower, but whatever he did made her the fastest home-grown 12-Metre in America in that summer of 1970. *Heritage* and *Weatherly* were eliminated early and *Valiant* proved no match for the revamped *Intrepid*, a 6–1 scoreline in favour of Chance's recreation putting her into the firing line with *Gretel II*.

The debate as to which of those two boats was the faster has never been heated; almost everyone is agreed that it was *Gretel II*, but that she was mismanaged is also universally accepted. Sir Frank Packer was still keen to justify his position as owner and he was calling the shots ashore which affected the running of the boat afloat. After the debacle of the first race, when *Gretel II*'s crew fouled up spinnaker hoists and had one man go over the side, Packer demanded that Jim Hardy should not be at

Sir James Hardy, Gilbert to his friends, who became fascinated with the 12-Metre class after reading the Lawson *History of the America's Cup*. He first raced for it in 1970 and has only missed involvement in one series since.

Intrepid was the first 12-Metre to have the rudder separated from the keel. Sparkman & Stephens retained some steering, together with variable keel section by maintaining a small trim-tab at the aft end of the keel. *Intrepid* was a two-time winner of the America's Cup and came close, in 1974, to defending for a third time.

the wheel for the start; instead he named Martin Visser for the job. His action at the start of the resailed second race led to the most acrimonious protest in the cup since Lord Dunraven accused the New York Yacht Club of cheating.

Alan Payne had done his homework before designing *Gretel II*. He knew the problems which Chance had thrown up with the 'bustle' around the stern of his designs and the associated amplified stern wave which it caused, and set out to master the 'separation effect' which was necessary. But he did not stop with hull research. Payne knew that the rig had to develop the maximum power with the least drag, and wind-tunnel tests pointed to this being improved with vortex generators on the mast. He therefore designed a rivet-fabricated – rather than welded – mast where the rivets were in exactly the

29

right place to double as vortex generators, such was his attention to fine detail. He even designed folding spreaders for the mast to allow the genoa to be sheeted closer. *Gretel II* had twin-wheel steering, which had the composite effect of allowing the helmsman to see the wave pattern to windward, and of sheeting the main boom in hard and low to accommodate the 'end plate' effect of the deck that Stephens had instituted with *Intrepid*.

Gretel II was undoubtedly fast and proved it by being the first to finish in that resailed second race. Then she was disqualified after the protest had been heard. Visser had hit *Intrepid* with *Gretel II*'s bow right under the noses of the NYYC Race Committee. The club received hundreds of letters accusing it of partiality while the press had a field day. The Australians bleated like stuck sheep but their knowledge of the racing rules was hopelessly exposed at the protest where *Intrepid*'s skipper, Bill Ficker, tore their argument to shreds. Time has healed the wound but the evidence was firmly in the American's favour.

Hardy might well have broken. He still says that afterwards he slept like a baby: 'I woke every two hours throughout the night and cried.' But Hardy is made of stout stuff, and even after losing the third race he pulled back from just over a minute down in the next to record his first win in a cup series. He lost the following race after leading because Ficker was that little bit cleverer in choosing when to tack. For the second time the slower 12-Metre had successfully defended the cup against the Australians.

It was the added experience of serious defender selection trials which honed Ficker, but that year was also the first of multiple challenges. Baron Bich was in Newport with two 12-Metres, *Chanceggar* and the André Mauric-designed *France*. *France* proved no match for *Gretel II* in their elimination series, and the Baron was so disappointed with the boat's performance that he sacked his skipper after three races and took the wheel himself for what

The Livingstone brothers, Frank and John, Australian sheep farmers and heavily committed anglophiles who funded *Kurrewa V* in 1964 in an effort to challenge for Britain and who helped Ian Howlett in his researches into 12-Metre design.

proved to be the last race. Newport's fog clamped down, reducing the visibility to 50 yards, and *Gretel II*, superbly navigated by Bill Fesq, found each of the marks while the Baron, with Eric Tabarly navigating for the first time, got totally lost and retired. The Race Committee should never have started that race; it was disgraceful that such an end to a well-planned and expensive challenge should have occurred.

Baron Bich then made the most magnanimous gesture to the Australians, putting *France* and *Chanceggar*, and their crews, at their disposal to prepare *Gretel II* for the cup races. Many 12-Metre observers regret the passing of those days, but 1970 marked the end of the beginning for the 12-Metre challenges for the America's Cup.

4 THE 1970s

The early 1970s were marked by the inconsequential threats of an America's Cup challenge from Britain, one which was never forthcoming and which did much to allow Alan Bond to make his first forays into the heady world of 12-Metres. The cup should have been held in 1973 and there were challenges from Canada, Britain, France, Italy and Australia, but those from Italy and Canada faded early. The Royal Thames Yacht Club asked for a year's delay and the New York Yacht Club was keen to grant it as many of its America's Cup Committee felt that there were more answers to come before the problems associated with the failure of *Valiant* could be eradicated. Then the British challenge failed completely and the Royal Thames was left with a certain amount of egg on its face and the duty of organising the challenger selection trials for *France* and *Southern Cross*.

This was also to be the era when 12-Metres began to be built of aluminium. Lloyd's, who control the scantlings of the class, took time to ensure that the wooden Twelves were not instantly outclassed, and to do so made the aluminium scantlings very generous. Bond was to build the world's first, a giant Twelve of more than 62,000 lbs displacement, to Bob Miller's designs (he was not then known as Ben Lexcen) with which the owner played publicity and secrecy against each other in an attempt to make the world pay attention to his campaign.

He could not, however, at first compete with Baron Bich. The Baron decided that he needed some extra assistance with his campaign and to that end enlisted the help of Paul Elvstrom. The four-times Olympic gold medallist was given full control of Bich's effort and took *France*, *Chanceggar* and *Constellation* to Denmark where he carried out his initial trials. He uprated *Constellation* to make her a

The greatest failure of all time was *Mariner*. The Britton Chance design was more than enough to have her crew saying rude things about her. The red-hulled *Mariner*, here just passing Castle Hill lighthouse, left Newport to be rebuilt and returned not much faster than she had been before.

faster yardstick for these trials, putting all her winches below deck and changing her wheel for a tiller. But the project went sour on Elvstrom, who was then an unwell man. The problems came to a head when *France* sank while under tow back to her native land from Denmark. In October 1973, with many innovative projects under way, including a very special mast, Bich terminated his arrangement with Elvstrom.

By then Bond had built his boat and was sailing it against *Gretel* and *Gretel II* off the Western Australian coast. The world's first aluminium 12-Metre, *Southern Cross*, had been placed in the hands of Olympic gold medallist John Cuneo, while her trial horse, *Gretel II*, was skippered by Jim Hardy. Bond, who had announced publicly that he would have a boatful of winners, found that Hardy was a better steerer of the boat than Cuneo but hesitated to make the change; Hardy, in his eyes, was a loser.

The oil crisis was having an effect on the American efforts. As the value of stocks plunged there were few millionaires who were prepared to swell the

Gretel II, undoubtedly faster than the Chance-altered *Intrepid* in 1970, but she was out-sailed by skipper 'Bus' Mossbacher and ruled out of one race by the protest committee.

A surprised Jim Hardy at a 1974 press conference in company with a bemused Ben Lexcen (then Bob Miller) explaining why *Southern Cross* had lost that day.

funds of the defending syndicates, and work on the latest Sparkman & Stephens design, *Courageous*, was stopped for ten days at Bill Strawbridge's request. Its effect was not so deleterious to the boat as to her afterguard. Bill Ficker was to have skippered her but when he heard of the cancellation of her building, he committed himself professionally and those commitments he had to honour. Bob Bavier, who had done it all before on *Constellation*, was persuaded to take over as skipper when building recommenced. It was to be a daunting summer for Bavier which was to end in his demise, at the eleventh hour, from the job. *Courageous* was to have more than her fair share of setbacks but not half the ones which the King's Point syndicate was to suffer.

There was no denying Britton Chance's talents; all round the world his designs were proving that he knew how to create fast boats. It was he who first approached George Hinman with the idea of forming a syndicate to build a boat of his design. Hinman had suffered with the Sparkman & Stephens-designed *Valiant* and was therefore susceptible to Chance's arguments. When Hinman named Ted Turner as the skipper, early on in the project, Chance was unhappy because he doubted whether Ted could win with a boat which gave him only a level opportunity. In his eyes Turner and many of his crew from the ocean-racing 12-Metre *American Eagle* were not into the finesse of America's Cup racing. To counter that, Chance believed, the only suitable tool would be a breakthrough boat, one which had sufficient extra speed to carry Turner to the front.

Somehow the path was not as clear as Britty had hoped. He was a month longer in the testing tanks than he should have been (and there are many who subsequently wondered whether he had consulted the results correctly) and it forced Bob Derecktor to a rushed building programme which saw the boat only two weeks late into the water. It was at her launch, when Turner saw Chance's creation for the first time, that the gap between skipper and designer widened visibly.

What Turner said when he saw the cut-off underbody of *Mariner* is part of sailing history, but as in so many other cases Turner gets the credit for what should have been attributed to someone else. It was not at the launch at all that Dennis Conner (not Turner) asked if anyone had seen fish with square tails but almost a month later when the crew were wet sanding the white bottom of the red-hulled *Mariner*. At the same time it was Legare Van Ness who remarked that even a turd is tapered.

Turner's real moment came much later. It was on 24 June, the first day of the NYYC's observation trials, the same day on which the Chance-designed *Ondine* beat the Bermuda Race record by two hours. *Mariner* had raced against her trial horse *Valiant* and beaten her by close to two minutes, and then drew *Intrepid* to race in the afternoon.

The cut-off stepped stern sections of *Mariner*, the Americans' failure in 1974. *Mariner* went back to her builders for radical surgery and these square ends disappeared.

36

Ted Turner relaxes on the dock at Goat Island Marina with a can of Iced Tea. In the early season *Mariner* and *Valiant* were moored here. It was before overnight hauling became *de rigueur*.

One can imagine the feeling when, for the first time, *Mariner* came up against *Intrepid*. Until then Ted Turner had had only the altered *Valiant* against which to judge the new boat's speed and he doubted whether, even altered, the flop of 1970 was a real yardstick. Dennis Conner was his tactician and, as they came out of the start, to windward of *Intrepid*, Turner asked him how they were going.

Conner: 'They're pointin' higher.'
Turner: (quizzically): 'Pointin' higher?'
Conner: 'And footin' faster.'
Turner: 'Pointin' higher and footin' faster. It's goin' to be a lawng summer!'

Intrepid sailed out from under *Mariner*'s lee and the writing was on the wall in big letters of the same colour as *Mariner*'s hull. Two days later *Mariner* was mauled by *Courageous* and still Turner could quip, 'The Germans were ahead in 1942,' but it had a hollow ring.

That year was one in which *Intrepid* was the dockside favourite. She was known as 'the People's Boat' and there were more than a few who were desirous of her making it 'Three Times a Lady'. It was also a year of bumper stickers in Newport. When *Mariner* went away to her builders for alterations to her stern, Turner had an aeroplane tow a banner proclaiming, '*Mariner* will return'; and a few days later a similar bumper sticker appeared with one wag's added comment: '– to the historic Mystic Seaport!'

Intrepid was a West Coast boat this time around. Gerry Driscoll had rebuilt her in his San Diego yard using Sparkman & Stephens designs which gave her a shape similar to her 1967 one but with input from the Lockheed tanks in California where larger models than the ones Chance had used for *Mariner* were able to be towed. Olin Stephens was also able to use this data for his design of *Courageous*. When *Mariner* and *Valiant* were eliminated the scene was set for the two-time cup winner to fight it out with her younger sister *Courageous*.

Courageous had her bad times and the afterguard changed right up to the last minute of the trials. Conner came in as starting helmsman and tactician after Ted Hood had been hired as upwind helmsman. Eventually there was nowhere for Bob Bavier to go but off the boat. Then ironically, with the scores level and the last trial race under way, *Intrepid* had her first gear failure of the season. A running backstay gave way on the first windward leg and the shock wave through the mast blew the hydraulic ram on the mast at deck level. The runner was repaired but the control of the mast had gone when the hydraulics failed and *Courageous* went on to win that trial and selection.

Twelve years later Gerry Driscoll still muses over how he was doubly robbed of a chance to defend the America's Cup: by the runner failure and, as he puts it, 'by a 13-Metre'. Well after the fate of the cup had been decided in 1974, Hood remeasured *Courageous* as part of his design research for *Independence* and found that she had been under-ballasted by 1,800 lbs when she met *Southern Cross*. When he heard about it, Alan Bond demanded the cup, but the officials at the New York Yacht Club could find no reason to part with it.

The other disappointed man of that summer was Ted Turner. He, however, made moves to buy, or at least have the right to sail, *Courageous* for the 1977 trials. Turner had tasted the bittersweet of America's Cup failure and he wanted success. On the West Coast, Lowell North was skippering a new Sparkman & Stephens 12-Metre, *Enterprise*, while Hood wanted a running mate for his *Independence*. Turner, with the right terms agreed, became that man, but only with the knowledge that, when the official trials began, he was in there with an equal chance. The heirarchy of the NYYC was hardly perturbed – there seemed little chance of Turner beating Hood and their real worry was that the 'upstarts' from the other side of the country might displace acknowledged order.

Above
The stern of *Southern Cross*, bearing as her hailing port 'Yanchep Sun City', an example of the signwriter's art which had the Royal Perth Yacht Club hierarchy up in arms at Alan Bond's commercialism. Yanchep Sun City eventually gave way, under pressure, to Fremantle.

Above left
Southern Cross, carefully watched in training by her nanny boat *Observer*.

Below left
It's not always light winds off Newport; *Intrepid* is running out to start the final trial, in 1974, against *Courageous*.

The West Coasters had *Intrepid* as a trial horse and Gerry Driscoll to sail her. Malin Burnham steered *Enterprise* when North was otherwise occupied, and the new boat's sail wardrobe did have a few experimental sails including a green 'garbage bag' genoa and a mainsail with a scalloped two-ply leech. The syndicate suffered from a lack of funds and was unable to take *Intrepid* to Newport for the cup summer.

Hood's boat suffered from a lack of speed: just that fraction of a knot which would have enabled her to beat *Courageous*. Turner had been expected to win in the early trials and then fade, but his final trials record of ten wins and one loss put the NYYC selectors in no doubt about his boat being the one to defend the cup for them, however much they would have preferred the establishment figure of Hood as their representative.

The characteristic stern of *Courageous* shows alongside her tender at the dockside at Newport. The 1974 Sparkman & Stephens design has been an active campaigner in five America's Cups.

40

Pelle Petterson steering *Sverige* with a tiller. His own-designed 12-Metre is one of the few in the class ever to have been so equipped.

That summer saw the introduction of a new country to cup racing. A Swedish commercial consortium funded the challenge of the Royal Goteberg Yacht Club with a boat designed and skippered by Pelle Petterson. *Sverige* had many different features, including tiller steering and her winches cranked, cycle-style, by the crew. Petterson was a known force in 6-Metre racing and an innovative designer, and *Sverige* proved a fast 12-Metre.

Bich was back too, but this time his effort had almost foundered before the trials began. His new *France 2* was found to be slower than her predecessor and special permission was given by the New York Yacht Club for some major rebuilding of the old boat in the United States to conform to the new 12-Metre rules. It took place during July and there was little chance for her crew to tune *France* prior to the challenger selection trials.

Jim Hardy and his brother Tom had failed to attract the necessary financial backing for a challenge and the one from the Eastern States of Australia resulted in *Gretel II* being altered after careful consideration by Alan Payne. She was fitted with an aluminium deck and optimised for light-weather performance after Gordon Ingate had purchased her from Alan Bond. Ingate and his crew were not in the first flush of youth – with little time at their disposal, Ingate went for experience – and they admitted it with T-shirts which warned: 'Daughters of America, lock up your mothers.'

Bond argued with his potential designers to such an extent that he called his challenge off for a period. Finally he agreed to go ahead with a boat jointly designed by Ben Lexcen and Johan Valentijn and there was little doubt which way they saw a winner. *Australia* was a short boat of light displace-ment with a big sail area – so big that the forestay was only a few inches from the stem and the boom almost overhung the aft deck. The lessons of previous cup races had been learned by both Australian challenges.

The constant campaigning during training races of *Gretel II* against *Southern Cross* undoubtedly improved the chances of the 1974 challenger, but the Americans had made even greater strides in 12-Metre designs.

Wearing the striped engineer's hat for which he has become famous, Ted Turner, the man who put his talent behind his mouth to come from underdog to conqueror in 1977.

Gary Jobson, the small boat champion who Turner chose to be his tactician in 1977 and who has been back for every America's Cup since.

The pattern of who was best soon began to emerge when the round-robin trials, organised by the Yacht Club d'Hyeres, got under way. The French were unable to win a race and met Australia in the semi-finals where the scoreline was 4–0 to the Aussies. However, *Gretel II* and *Sverige* were much more evenly matched, their semi-final going to a seventh race, and only then did *Sverige* beat the older boat. In the final selection trials Noel Robins and his crew executed a carefully controlled dismissal of *Sverige* by winning the first four races, the scoreline exaggerating the Australian's superiority.

That fact was proved by Turner. He knew that he had a faster boat and let Robins win starts in order that he could stay out of trouble. His tactician, Gary Jobson, many years later says that he would have loved to be roughing it up with the Australians but admits that there was really no need. *Courageous* was slightly faster and Turner took advantage of it.

Courageous approaching the America's Cup buoy for a down-wind finish in one of her 1974 races against *Intrepid*.

Australia provided a big surprise by beating *Freedom* in one light-air race and by being well ahead of her in another when the time-limit ran out.

Russell Long, skipper of *Clipper*, wanted to take his yacht to the '79 World Championship but was refused permission by the New York Yacht Club.

Tom Blackaller, twice world champion of the Star class and lover of fast cars and women, began a flirtation with the 12-Metres in 1980 and cannot kick the habit.

Left
Australia starts in an easterly breeze using the flatter of her two mainsails cut for the bendy mast. The choice that day proved to be a mistake.

His performance at the final press conference may not have been what the NYYC would have liked; Turner had done justice to the bottle of aquavit which the Swedes had given him and just about anything else he could lay his hands on before going to the Armory to tell all. Each time he opened his mouth, either to speak or to swig on the Swede's bottle, it was to tumultuous cheers. Turner was king and already talking of being back in three years' time.

He kept his word, returning with the same boat, the same eleven in her crew – but without the same fire in the belly which is necessary to win the cup. In all truth what had happened was that Denis Conner had changed the game. With West Coast money he took over *Enterprise* and had Sparkman & Stephens design *Freedom* for him. Then he proceeded to sail the 12-Metres for 300 days a year for three years. Turner viewed this attitude as unworthy: 'The man's got nothing better to do.' It was, however, a telling play which provided Conner with a perfectly prepared craft and a well-documented loft of sails (over ninety bags full) to power her. He swept to victory in the defender selection trials, suffering only three defeats in the whole summer.

The challenge to Conner came not from Turner and *Courageous* but from Russell Long and *Clipper*. Long had taken over *Independence* the previous year and the yacht saw a metamorphosis when David Pedrick drew some new lines and it was decided to cut her deck and upper 6 inches of topsides away and put the new hull underneath. That done, the ceremony for the launch of the boat was only a day away when Long had commercial sponsorship from Pan-Am confirmed. Instead of being *Eagle*, *US 32* became an overnight signwriter's nightmare changing to *Clipper*.

Long recruited the services of Tom Blackaller in mid-season and his known rivalry with Conner was bound to create some aggression. It did, but not enough to master a Conner with three years' drive behind him.

Sverige was back at Newport three years on but with a slightly lower-key operation, while Baron Bich put his eggs into a new basket. *France 3* was designed by Valentijn and had Bruno Trublé to steer her. Trublé's record in other classes was sufficient to give him credence in this ethereal world and he also had the confidence of the Baron, a necessary attribute to keep his hands on the wheel throughout the summer.

Lexcen had reworked *Australia* and Noel Robins had given way to Jim Hardy, but when the boat arrived in Newport the locals could have been forgiven for wondering if the Australians were serious. The paint job was dreadful and three weeks' hard work was necessary by her crew before she was ready for racing. She had a new keel and was about to sprout a new and radical mast, a fact which not even Lexcen knew at that time.

The mast came after Lexcen had seen the spar which the British boat *Lionheart* began to use when the challenger selection trials were about to start. Oakeley and Howlett had plotted that a bigger and more efficient mainsail could be set on a spar which had considerable fore-and-aft bend in its upper half. They tried to keep their secret weapon to themselves, but once it appeared in Newport there was no containing the outside interest, nor stopping anyone from copying or improving on it. The bendy mast had such an advantageous effect on *Lionheart*'s performance that Lexcen did what any red-blooded designer would have done: he locked himself away until he had designed one similar – not, it must be added, until a thirty-page French protest (inspired by the Americans) had been heard to decide the legality of such a spar. Then he personally supervised the building of this mast which was not stepped until after *Australia* had won the challenger selection trials.

It was a summer of dissent and Newport was shaken when Oakeley was fired by the British syndicate. The row had been brewing for some time; Oakeley had refused to alter the shape of

Above
With a Kevlar/Mylar mainsail set on the bendy mast copied from *Lionheart*, *Australia* was a much more potent performer.

Below
Southern Cross leads *France* across the starting line at one of the final trials in 1974.

Overleaf
Courageous won the cup in 1974 with Ted Hood as skipper; she won it again in 1977 with Ted Turner at the wheel and was a serious challenge candidate again in 1980. Never suppressed, *Courageous*, skippered by John Kolius, gave Dennis Conner many uneasy moments in 1983.

Lionheart's afterguard, claiming that he did not need a tactician as well as a navigator; they were two roles which, with modern instrumentation, he saw as one. The syndicate chiefs demurred and finally gave him the option of falling in line or getting out. For Oakeley, principles were paramount.

Lawrie Smith took over as skipper of Lionheart and was woefully short of experience in sailing boats of this size. He did, however, give it his best shot and might well have levelled the series with France 3 but for the decision of the jury on a starting-line protest in the sixth race. It went against the British and forms a classic 'test case' in yachting law. Meanwhile the Australians were slaying the Swedes, after a two-day halt caused by the snapping of Australia's Mark 3 Lexcen mast when a spreader collapsed. Then Hardy made relatively short work of the French, losing one race only when he sailed into a hole and Troublé, from being eight minutes' down, went on to win.

Bruno Troublé steers France 3, the Lexcen and Valentijn design, prior to the start of an elimination race.

Lawrie Smith took over as skipper of Lionheart from John Oakeley in 1980, skippered Victory '83 in the cup races of 1983 and has been nominated by the Royal Torbay Yacht Club syndicate to be their skipper in 1990.

Clipper began life as *Independence*, the hull was totally rebuilt leaving only the deck intact, and was to have been called *Eagle*. Last-minute sponsorship by Pan-Am gave the signwriters an overnight job before her launching.

Lexcen hardly gave his sail makers the time to make a mainsail to fit the bendy mast and for five days the Australians did their best to make the mast and sails work. There was a new noise in the boat as the leech of the mainsail shook in anything over 15 knots of breeze, but Benny had gambled and around him the rest beavered to make his ideas come to fruition. He had aimed to be superfast in light weather and all he needed was for Aeolus to answer his prayers.

However, they went unheeded for the first race when, in 12 knots, Conner won going away. But all was not as rosy in the American camp as it might have been; *Freedom* had had a gear breakdown during the race when the steering failed on the second beat. Conner had had to steer the boat using only the trim tab until a jury control on the rudder quadrant was effected with lines to the winches.

The second race was the one to show the Americans that they were no longer omnipotent in 12-Metre racing. *Freedom* led around the first four marks, but when the 6-knot wind faded away *Australia* went past and built a huge lead. Her victory was only stopped when the five-and-a-half-hour time limit ran out. When the race was resailed, again in 6 knots or so of breeze, Hardy led at the weather mark after outpointing and outfooting Conner. With but one hiccup on the first reach, *Australia* went on to record the first win for a challenger since Hardy had won with *Gretel II* ten years earlier. After that, things went *Freedom*'s way. She won the third race by just under a minute and the fourth one, when Australia chose the wrong (small) mainsail, by nearly four minutes.

The weather became the important feature of the match and Conner, hearing the forecast of light winds for the next day, called for a lay-day. The move was correct. That lay-day was one of light and shifting winds in Newport Sound, exactly what the Australians would have chosen. The following day the wind was up to 12–15 knots and the Australians lost the race and the cup as *Freedom* ran away from her opponent.

Conner had shown the world the way to win the America's Cup. No longer was it sufficient to be in Newport for a single summer: the road to the Holy Grail was a three-year trudge with every possible hour packed with practice and still more practice. The fun was draining out of the cup, but there was more life than ever before in the 12-Metre Class.

Above
The 1980 British challenger, *Lionheart*, was skippered by John Oakeley until a major policy breakdown with syndicate chiefs. Oakeley was fired the day after he had won two races in the elimination series.

Below
Dennis Conner always appeared to have superiority over Jim Hardy at the start of the 1980 races. *Freedom*, one of the best prepared defenders of all time, took the series by four races to one.

5 ANYWHERE BUT NEWPORT, OR ALMOST

Left
Sverige at Brighton.

Below
*France 3, Lionheart,
Clipper, Australia* and
Victory at the start of the
third race of the Rolex
World Cup in Newport,
1982.

The America's Cup so dominated the 12-Metre Class that Newport, Rhode Island, was the only place where 12-Metres were sailed in competition for many years. The Americans, the New York Yacht Club particularly, made such a fetish of not racing anyone else except for the cup that the class achieved the status of the dinosaur – overbred and undernourished. The paucity of new boats was the direct result of the lack of use: unless the cup was the aim, there was nothing for a 12-Metre to do except be parked in a line in the shed at Cove Haven to await another cup summer, possibly as a trial horse or, failing that, to be sold for conversion as an ocean-racing cruiser.

Above
Phil Crebbin at the wheel of *Victory* in Newport. A year later Crebbin was fired from the skipper's role in a minor 'palace revolution', despite being de Savary's nominated skipper from the outset.

Left
The evergreen *Columbia*, then twenty-one years old, skippered by John Caulcutt, racing in the 1979 World Championships.

Overleaf
The highlight of the 1979 World Championship was the close racing between John Oakeley in *Lionheart* and Pelle Petterson in *Sverige*.

Even in Newport there was nothing in the way of competition except in the cup summers and that was reserved for the American boats. Not until the multiple challenges began in 1970 was there anything other than trialling for the foreign boats, except the New York Yacht Club's oddly named Cruise, and that became barred to non-American boats.

In the winter of 1978, with *Lionheart* building, John Oakeley suggested to Pelle Petterson that both might benefit if the two met in friendly competition. The lessons of the American competition in the defender selection trials had been obvious to Oakeley when he watched the 1977 cup races. They agreed to meet for some racing in Sweden's Marstrand Fiord in June but the logistics of getting *Lionheart* into battle were fearsome.

There was no spare budget to ship the boat to Sweden and the only alternative was to sail her there. To do so John Giblet prepared her with

temporary hatch covers of thick plywood that could be pulled down on to a rubber seal. The accommodation was rudimentary – hammocks were slung inside the cavernous aluminium hull which had been stuffed with all the sails which *Lionheart* had in her small wardrobe – and the passage one which Giblet and his crew will never look back on with much favour. Cooking was performed on a small camping gas stove with two burners – just enough power to feed the seven-man crew – and the passage of more than 1,000 miles was achieved in five days through a fair amount of fog.

Above
Rod Davis, twice winner of the Congressional Cup, uses his 'Italian connections' to great advantage. They enabled him to sail aboard the Yacht Club Italiano's entries in both the 1984 and 1986 World Championships prior to his skippering a challenge for the Newport Harbor Yacht Club syndicate in 1987.

Left
Lionheart, on starboard tack, crosses ahead of *Sverige* shortly before the latter's mast fell down for the second time at Brighton 1979.

Right
On *Sverige*'s bow two crewmen prepare the genoa for hoisting and in the light winds *Gretel II* is ahead.

Overleaf, left
There is an elegance all its own about the 12-Metre rig. *Sverige* has the perfect match of mainsail and genoa, a parallel 'slot' is maintained between the two sails.

Overleaf, right
Victory heading towards overall success in the Rolex World Cup.

Once in Marstrand, Oakeley and his crew set about the task of taking on the highly experienced Swedes. Petterson and his crew had been through a complete cup summer in Newport and knew the ins and outs of match racing, even if they were a touch rusty. *Lionheart* took the first shortened series for the GKSS Cup and reached a 4–4 state in the second series, an eleven-match affair, for the Marstrand Cup. There had been no clear leader in the 12½-mile races, first *Lionheart* winning and then *Sverige*. The only problem was fog which occasionally clamped in and made finding the marks difficult.

It stopped the tenth race of the series after *Lionheart* had added another win to her score, and by the staggering margin of over six minutes. The following day the British boat finished her racing in Sweden with a flourish. In light-to-moderate

Overleaf
Azzurra (I 4) leads (from left) *Victory '83*, *Canada 1* and *Challenge 12* in the 1984 World Championship.

Right
During the '82 World Cup *Australia* was skippered by syndicate head Peter de Savary until he fouled *France 3*, breaking a foot or so from *Australia*'s bow and putting a large hole in the port side of *France 3*.

The crew of *France 3* have more than a handful as they douse the spinnaker to start the second beat in a World Cup '82 race.

Gretel II wearing her latest finery to compete as a fifteen-year-old in the World Championships at Porto Cervo.

Overleaf, left
The moment of trip as the bowman of *Victory '83* lets go the windward clew of the spinnaker prior to a take-down.

Overleaf, right
The crew of *Courageous II* preparing to gybe in the Great Sound, Bermuda, during winter training in December 1984.

Left
Despite its latitude Nassau can be cool in winter, but 12-Metre training has to continue no matter what the weather.

Below
Nassau made an ideal winter training ground for the *Victory* syndicate, although returning the boats through shallow water in the late evening was slightly hazardous.

breezes the Ian Howlett-designed heavy-displacement 12-Metre won the two races to take home the Marstrand Cup. For John Giblet and a small crew, there was the long sail home. They set out into a force 6–7 wind and, once into the North Sea, hove to with a staysail and the short hoist mainsail. Giblet's memories are of a 'wet, wet trip'. Their only consolation was a gallon jar of Black & White Whisky which the distillery had donated for the passage!

Both Oakeley and Petterson were agreed that the two series had been useful in their preparation for the main event and that another meeting should take place as soon as possible. Oakeley's sponsoring club, the Royal Southern Yacht Club, had arranged, with the financial backing of a local television company, to run the 12-Metre World Championship off Brighton. The huge marina complex there was ideal for a 12-Metre regatta and the match racing was preceded by one race in which seven boats took part. *War Baby*, the converted *American Eagle*, was not up to the rest of the Twelves and many of those were long in the tooth.

Overleaf
Freedom squeezes between *Azzurra* and *Canada 1* on her way to the weather mark as the others head off on the first reach of a World Championship course.

Left
An apprehensive Damian Fewster on the bow of *Challenge 12* feeding the last of the genoa luff into the headfoil as she approaches the leeward mark in a 1984 Championship race, just to the leeward of *New Zealand*, which is steered by Chris Dickson.

Constellation and *Columbia* were older than *Gretel II* and *Windrose* (the former *Chanceggar*), and only *Lionheart* and *Sverige* could aptly be described as being up-to-date. The championship was none the worse for its predictable outcome and more than a few sailors had their first taste of 12-Metre racing off Brighton. *Lionheart* won, aided somewhat by *Sverige* twice losing her mast over the side.

The International Yacht Racing Union was not prepared to grant world championship status to an event in Newport in September 1982, knowing perhaps that the USA would boycott it. One American, however, did wish to race but was warned off by the New York Yacht Club; even when he wanted to charter *Intrepid* from the Canadians, Tom

Against what many felt was ill-judgment, the *Victory* syndicate chose to take *Australia* (K 212) and *Lionheart* (K 21) to the Bahamas for the winter. The argument against *Lionheart* was that she was hardly characteristic of the type of 12-Metre which would be sailed the following summer.

There can be sunny days too, and the racing was close between *Lionheart* and *Australia* in the rolling seas to the north of New Providence Island.

Blackaller was told not to. The event, the Rolex World Cup, became a benefit for the de Savary *Victory* syndicate. It had entered three of the five boats, but the less said the better about the antics of the syndicate head in Australia in the final race – when on port tack he T-boned *France 3*.

That race was won by *Lionheart* with Lawrie Smith and Rodney Pattisson in control. *Victory*, the Dubois-designed Twelve, won two races, as did *Clipper* in the hands of the Canadians, while *Australia* won the other. On points it was *Victory*'s cup and, strangely enough, her last race. From there she went for alterations but internal politics in the de Savary camp kept her out of competitive sailing, even as a trial horse for her younger sister. No one will ever know if she was much faster for her alterations.

The *Victory* syndicate carried on training through the winter and chose Nassau as the place to do it. The weather was not what its members might have wanted: there was more wind than they would have liked, but it did give the shore staff some unwanted

practice in fixing bent and broken masts. Using *Australia* and *Lionheart*, the sailing was mostly for crew-training purposes and for sail evaluation. But should you have to sail through the winter there are far worse places than Nassau, and as a venue for 12-Metre competition it could rate high if the Americans were prepared to try it.

On the other hand, there is Bermuda, which Leonard Greene's *Courageous* syndicate chose for winter training soon after the America's Cup went down under. *Courageous* was fitted with a Greene-designed Vortex Wing (Greene's trademarked title) keel and, with *Defender*, there was every chance of a good start to the campaign. As a trial ground for Fremantle, Bermuda certainly boasts sufficient similarities in wind and wave conditions to make it worthwhile for any 12-Metre with a yearning for good living.

Triple Olympic medallist Rodney Pattisson took over with Lawrie Smith as joint skipper for the *Victory* syndicate on Crebbin's demise.

Below
Dennis Conner steers the then Italian-owned *Freedom* to chase *Victory '83*, also in Italian hands, off Porto Cervo.

The Yacht Club Italiano
became very serious with
its challenge for the
America's Cup, and
bought *Victory '83*. Here
she is crossed by
Challenge 12, purchased
by another Italian
syndicate which failed to
raise the necessary
finance to carry its
challenge to Australia.

6 SECRECY

There has always been tremendous satisfaction in playing a trump card late in the game, and the big yachting events are no different from any other major sporting event in this respect. Upsetting the play by pre-empting or by reducing the odds is another familiar ploy of sailors. When Sir T.O.M. Sopwith agreed to let sailmakers Ratsey's experiment with a quadrilateral headsail for *Endeavour* in 1934, the trials were held well inside the Solent with the eyes of the world's yachtsmen upon the new creation. In no time at all *Rainbow* was sporting one off Newport.

The British should have learned their lesson. *Shamrock IV* was on her way to America when the First World War was declared and American naval architects had four years to examine the lines of the Charles Nicholson design. Had they been kept under wraps, the history of the America's Cup might have been very different.

In the early days of the 12-Metres, secrecy was kept until boats were launched. No one then felt that there was much that their rivals could do. The sunken crew deck of *Sceptre* took all the world by surprise. Nobody had talked to the workers in Robertson's Clydeside shed or they could easily have found out what was going on. Nearly thirty years later anyone who works on a 12-Metre has to sign an agreement that they will not reveal anything about the boat; one foundry worker tried, unsuccessfully, to sell the keel plans of *Crusader* to the New York Yacht Club for $20,000, the price he put on the technological advancement in 1985.

When Baron Bich entered the scene, he commissioned Britton Chance Jnr to design a 12-Metre which was to be built by Eggar in Switzerland, thus doubly disqualifying it from being used in the

The cockpits of 12-Metres are ergonomically designed but not everyone is in agreement as to what is best. From the bottom *Azzurra, Freedom, France 3, Canada 1* and *Challenge 12.*

The winglets from *Victory '83*'s keel, removed after their value was considered dubious.

Left
The keel that changed the face of history – Ben Lexcen's winged wonder disguised by blue paint in the areas where it failed to conform to the norm.

America's Cup. Bich's advisers threw a security screen around the boat and no one was allowed inside the yard where she was being built – it was the first time that there had ever been such overtly tight secrecy.

Journalist Jack Knights was determined to find out what was going on and what shape Chance had drawn for the Baron. To that end Knights climbed the barbed-wire fence in the middle of one night, ripping his trousers in the process, and with camera in hand walked into the shed to claim his scoop. There were no night security staff around and, at the cost of a new pair of pants, Knights found out what he wanted to know.

I thought of him six years later in Newport when I went in search of information, also in the middle of the night and also faced with a barbed-wire fence. I had got wind of a magical device that was being used aboard *Courageous*, about which none of her crew

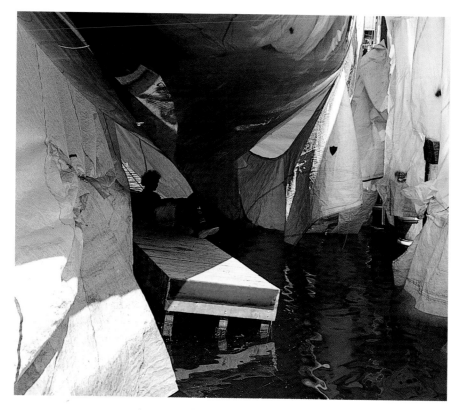

David Woolner surrounded by a temporary screen while removing the winglets from the keel of *Victory '83*.

were prepared to talk but about which plenty of rumour was circulating. It was suggested that she had an on-board computer which provided her afterguard with rapid information about the true wind speed and direction, and navigational data that no one had ever had before.

Courageous came out of the water – overnight resting in hoists was not a regular feature of 1974 – for some work to be carried out on her bottom about a month before the cup, when she was still involved in selection trials with *Intrepid*. I noticed her in the yard near the Goat Island bridge, and the temptation became overwhelming. I excused myself early from David Ray's famous Newport watering hole, the Candy Store, went to bed and set my alarm for 0330.

Dressed in dark slacks and a black sweater, I drove down to the yard and parked close to the fence so that the car would provide me with a start to climbing over it. I took with me a camera with flash-gun, torch and notebook. Straddling the fence, I remembered Knights and took great care. Once in the yard I found a short ladder and climbed into

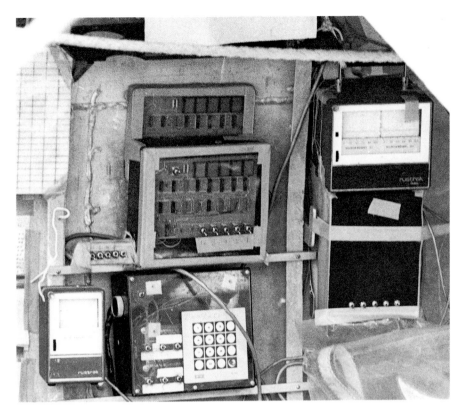

Sidney Greybox, the first computer to be found on board a 12-Metre. This Data General 1200, modified for *Courageous* in 1974 by Rich McCurdy, was part of her winning strategy.

Overleaf
Eight 12-Metres hang in the specially constructed hoists at the Aga Khan's Centre in Porto Cervo. From the far end they are: *Victory '83, Gretel II, Challenge 12, Canada 1, France 3, New Zealand* (ex *Enterprise), Freedom* and *Azzurra.*

Courageous, under the tarpaulin with which she was covered to keep the rain out. Down below I headed for the navigation station to meet Sidney Greybox.

Named after his casing, Sidney was a much modified Data General Nova 1200 mini-computer which the *Courageous* syndicate had installed as an alternative to running a trial horse throughout the summer. The syndicate felt that the alternative was cheaper and more accurate. To modify the computer and to make it effective for their purposes, they appointed Rich McCurdy of the Kenyon Instrument Company as consultant, and it was he who considered Sidney his baby.

I pointed the torch at the schedule taped to the side of the boat which listed Sidney's various functions and wrote them down in my notebook. I set my camera and twice photographed the entire set-up; it seemed like three years while the flashgun recharged. Then it was out of the boat and back over the fence, taking great care not to catch anything on the barbed wire, and away to my bed.

Some four hours later I headed for a breakfast bar, only to sit alongside Rich McCurdy at the counter.

We exchanged pleasantries and the conversation drifted, inevitably, around to the computer on *Courageous*. Rich did not seem to mind that I made notes as we went along, and as we finished our meal he said, 'Do you want to come over to see it? Bring your camera with you.' I have never dared to tell him what I was doing a few hours before!

For years security was nothing more than making 'non-family' stay at a reserved distance. Boats were hung out to dry but the docks were the province of the syndicate members; you could take photographs of the boats with long-focal-length lenses and study the pictures at leisure, but unless you were part of that campaign you were rarely allowed close. It was a well-observed truce that every red-blooded reporter sought to break.

The scene changed dramatically when *Australia II* arrived in Newport for the summer of 1983. She was constantly surrounded in shrouding – a 'modesty skirt' some called it – and there was no getting past

The security screen on the starboard side of *Spirit of America* hides only the profile shape of her keel as she is lowered into the water . . .

the armed guard at the end of the dock. A couple of Canadians tried to look at the keel, and photograph it, by arriving underwater. They were caught and their film was confiscated, but unknown to them they had been beaten to the draw. *Australia II* had not been two days in Newport before one syndicate knew, in some detail, what Alan Bond had to hide.

Many 12-Metre experts believe that Bond may live to regret the grand gesture he made on 26 September 1983 when he raised both arms to tell the hoist driver to bring *Australia II* out of the water and show the world her keel after she had won the America's

. . . a longer lens shows greater detail of the bustle shape of *Spirit* in her original, heavy-displacement form.

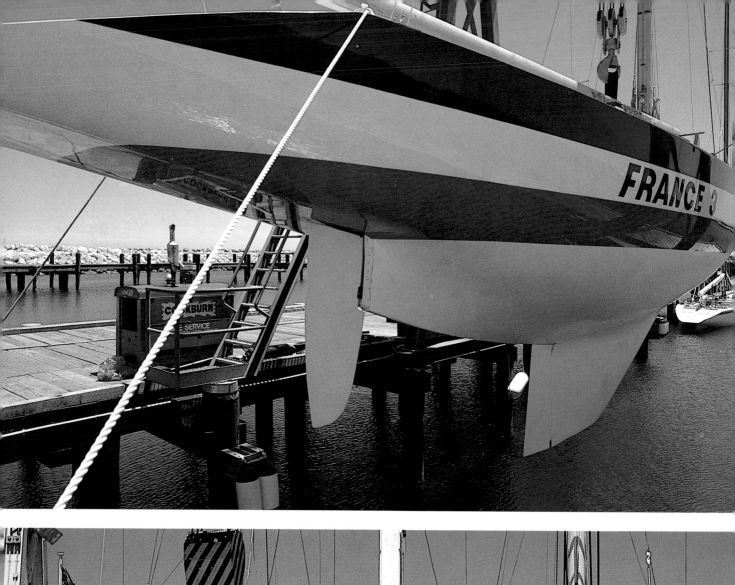

Cup. The technological difference between his boat and all the other 12-Metres then in the world was huge. Bond's gesture revealed exactly what Ben Lexcen had done and put the rest of the world at the same starting point for the 1987 America's Cup. It would be, arguably, difficult for the same designer to make two quantum jumps in an historically well-researched area.

Australia II now hangs daily in her hoist at the Bond headquarters in Mews Road, Fremantle: the benchmark of 12-Metre design. Alongside her throughout the summer of 1985/6 was her younger sister, *Australia III*, the larger part of her underbody screened from prying eyes.

Australia III was not alone. The pendulum had swung the other way and the oddities were those which were on view. The New Zealanders, dashing into the America's Cup for the first time, had a refreshingly honest and open approach. They welcomed people into their compound to see the world's first two glassfibre 12-Metres while the World Championship was on. They claimed they had nothing to hide, but their boats were very different from all the others around and when their three designers come up with their final offering for the America's Cup 1987, *New Zealand 7* could well have a screen around her underwater surfaces.

7 THE 1983 AMERICA'S CUP

From the very start of the cup summer of 1983 it was readily apparent that there was a shift in the balance of power. There were more than twice as many challengers as defenders and the challenging boats would have more racing, and therefore more match practice, than the three defending boats. In the past the strength of the American defence had been in the heavy competition which the successful defender had to overcome; this time there was a paucity of competition in the home side.

In the very early stages it was obvious that *Defender* was not going to set the world alight. Tom Blackaller and Gary Jobson had induced Nick and Jane Heyl to fund the Dave Pedrick-designed 12-Metre, and even as she hit the water *Defender* was unable to beat the 1974-designed *Courageous*. David Vietor, who was the Svengali of this syndicate, was aware that this was likely from velocity prediction programmes of the two boats which he had commissioned, and theoretical alterations to *Courageous* always seemed to help her more than similar alterations to *Defender*. Yet during her life *Defender* experienced may alterations under the chainsaw and welding torch, and several changes of ballast and sail plan in an effort to gain speed.

In the winter of 1982/3 in California, *Defender* began to get the better of *Courageous*, even when John Kolius and John Bertrand joined her afterguard. It was the high point of her career, because when she was trucked back to Newport for the cup summer, *Defender* was found not to be a 12-Metre by quite a margin on being measured. More surgery did make her the desired length but did not result in the desired speed, despite the fact that in her new state she had more sail and more ballast. Blackaller always blames the original dearth of money for

The urbanity of John Bertrand, 'Mr Clean', was just one of the attributes which helped him to become the winning skipper in 1983. In his speech accepting the cup outside the former Vanderbilt mansion, Bertrand was both serious and witty, but afloat his prime asset was determination.

Left
On board *France 3* Bruno Troublé and his crew make last-minute adjustments in search of speed.

95

Defender's lack of speed, believing that the shortage led to a cheapskate operation which reflected badly. Whatever it was, she did not give Blackaller and Jobson a very happy summer.

Courageous too had her bad times. The July trials saw her win only two races and lose thirteen, but her losses could never be described as serious ones. In the cruel reality of the selection trials, however, any loss is a bad one, although Kolius was proving to be a good 12-Metre skipper. Vietor had always had confidence in the design of *Courageous*: he had twice suggested to aspiring syndicate heads that they buy her as a starting point; and his confidence became realised as the summer wore on and the boat began to obtain a reasonable wardrobe of sails.

Defender was the first of the pair to be eliminated as *Courageous* began a period of marked improvement. But if *Courageous* were showing this well, the question which was being asked all over Newport was, 'Just how good is *Liberty*?'

The 1983 cup provided John Kolius with an opportunity to shine and he took it with both hands. For a time it appeared that, against the odds, he might take *Courageous* to her third defence.

Right
Jack Sutphen at the wheel of *Freedom* provides the bench mark during speed trials for Dennis Conner and *Magic*.

A typical day in Newport Sound – *Challenge 12* and *Australia II* await the sea breeze.

As soon as the breeze comes the 12-Metres spring to life. *Australia II*, with her light-weather sails hoisted, settles down prior to the pre-start manoeuvres.

Dennis Conner had begun his campaign by order-
ing two 12-Metres to be designed and built, the only
criterion being that they had to be faster than
Freedom. One, *Spirit of America*, was designed by
Sparkman & Stephens, while the other, *Magic*, came
from the board of Johan Valentijn. They were as
unalike as it is possible for two boats built to the
same rule to be: *Spirit* was a big vessel, moderately
heavy in displacement and short on sail, while *Magic*
was a tiny craft which took penalties in several areas.

Conner raced the two boats against each other
and it was not until the summer of 1982 that he raced
either of them against *Freedom*. He had already
found that *Magic* was the slower and so decided to
test *Spirit* against *Freedom* first. The difference was
amazing and it was not good for Conner: *Freedom*
was markedly superior. Valentijn convinced Conner
to cut the back end off *Magic* and replace it with a
new one, but that made little difference; neither did
the changes which Sparkman & Stephens made to
Spirit.

None of this helped to generate goodwill between the two designers, and when Valentijn was asked to co-operate with Sparkman & Stephens, he quit the project. Conner, not wanting to lose him, therefore swung his design campaign fully towards the former Dutchman, now a naturalised American, and in doing so shut out Sparkman & Stephens completely. It was, however, close to panic time – and a syndicate without a fast 12-Metre is an undesirable embarrassment.

Liberty was never much faster than *Freedom* and often the older boat had the edge, but when they modified her, Conner and Valentijn inadvertently stopped her from being a 12-Metre. Changes in the rules had penalised her low freeboard but that penalty was not applied, under a 'grandfathering' clause, if the hull shape was maintained, but when Valentijn altered the bow and the rudder and shifted the ballast, he had lost the penalty block and taken *Freedom* out of the running for the trials.

It would have been beneficial to the American cause to have *Freedom* race in the selection trials rather than to have one boat sit it out each day. That was not in Dennis Conner's mind, however. He had planned to race *Freedom* in the July trials while alterations were made to *Liberty*, but the plan blew up in his face. What he did have, as a game plan, was the ability to alter *Liberty*'s sail area:displacement ratio rapidly to meet any of three measurement certificates. It meant that, to all intents and purposes, she was three different boats to meet varying conditions, a state of affairs which was to suffer severe criticism from challengers and defenders alike.

The challengers began to gather in Newport early. Some, like the French, the Canadians and Peter de Savary's *Victory* syndicate, had been there in 1982, gone south to Florida or the Bahamas for the winter, and returned for the cup summer.

In Australia the Melbourne syndicate's *Challenge 12* had given *Australia II* a fair run for her money and there were those who honestly believed that the earlier Lexcen design had considerable untapped

Challenge 12 (to windward) and *Advance* were among the first three (with *France 3*) to be eliminated from the Challenger Selection Trials in 1984.

potential. She suffered in Newport from a lack of funds, which was reflected in her sail wardrobe. Had she had the new sails, she would not have been among the first to be eliminated from the challenger selection trials. Syndicate head Dick Pratt made a valiant attempt to put the fun back into the America's Cup with a dinner at one of Newport's mansions. It backfired horribly.

He had invited former Australian prime minister Malcolm Fraser to speak and Fraser had taken the line that the heritage of America and Australia had a great deal in common in that they were both founded by 'English undesirables', adding that the most undesirables were still left in England. It caused the odd titter but more embarrassment than amusement as the Marchioness of Milford Haven was among those present, and Fraser went on later to say that if anyone thought he should apologise he was not going to.

The evening went from bad to worse when Aussie comic Campbell McComas, in a satirical review of the America's Cup and its protagonists, made a snide remark at New York Yacht Club vice-commodore and former cup-winning skipper 'Bus' Mosbacher. Mrs Mosbacher stood up with the retort, 'I've had enough,' and swept out with her husband.

Despite the interruptions the evening continued and when the time came for me to make my way to my valet-parked moped, I paused to thank my host and add that I had enjoyed myself, 'even though I am a Pom!' Fraser, who was standing alongside Dick Pratt, gloated: 'I wonder you didn't leave.' I just could not resist the counter: 'No sweat. I've been insulted by experts. I don't take any notice of has-beens!'

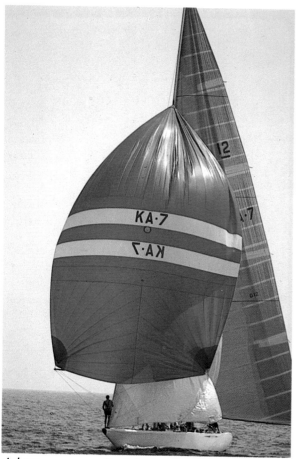

Advance was a radical design by Alan Payne but was never up to the pace of her contemporaries. Her crew painted the black nose on the 'dog' to show that it was of good pedigree and relatively healthy.

With one day still left in the 1983 America's Cup, the Italians, eliminated in the Challenger semi-finals, folded their tents and left for home. *Azzurra* travelled on one of her sponsor's trucks.

Mauro Pellaschier skippered *Azzurra* to an outstanding first run for the Italians in the America's Cup.

From the outset of the *Victory* campaign Phil Crebbin was the nominated skipper, that is, until he was axed from the programme just before the Challenger semi-final trials began.

Challenge 12 soon became a has-been too – eliminated from the challenger trials before the semi-finals. With her went *Advance*, the 12-Metre designed by Alan Payne for the Syd Fischer-headed Royal Sydney Yacht Squadron syndicate. *Advance* lacked money and time, and also further design input which she was denied. Iain Murray had a stab at making her go, but without success. She was an acknowledged 'dog' and her crew painted the first foot or so of her bow in black gloss because, as they said, 'every dog should have a wet and shiny nose!'

The third of the seven to be eliminated was *France 3*. The 1980 Valentijn design was modified by Jacques Faroux, but like the others who suffered the same fate, she was woefully short of sails and the other 'goodies' that are excluded from a low-budget campaign.

The *Azzurra* syndicate was never short of funds. This Italian group, headed by the Aga Khan, had a budget of more than $5 million. It was enough for the Italians, who had bought *Enterprise* as their benchmark, to do relatively well with their Andrea Vallicelli-designed boat, but towards the end of the campaign they wilted under pressure.

Canada 1 wilted even faster in the final stages. The oilmen from Calgary, who began the challenge from the Secret Cove Yacht Club, never did quite honour their promises of sufficient funds to run it well. The Canadians had few good sails and a definite down-side on masts and rigging. It was another of those might-have-been campaigns.

Nothing was stinted by de Savary for the British effort, except the decision as to who was to be in charge of the boat. He insisted that the final choice would not be made until the last moment. De Savary had two boats and two crews working all the time, but it soon became obvious that he could not go on using Phil Crebbin, Lawrie Smith and Rodney Pattisson without making the choice as to who was number one. The internecine warfare was not pretty and finally it was Crebbin who was chopped from the programme.

Victory '83 was designed by Ian Howlett as a successor to the Ed Dubois *Victory*, and her performance improved throughout the summer. She was a notably good performer in light weather conditions and, indeed, defeated *Australia II* in the first of their final eliminations in just those circumstances. After that, however, *Australia II* took the next four races to become the twenty-fifth challenger for the America's Cup.

There was much that *Australia II*, her crew, her designer and her owner had to suffer before her path was clear to the cup. There was the matter which became known as 'Keelgate'. Did Ben Lexcen design her winged keel or was it the work of a Dutchman? Lexcen, and Alan Bond, held that it was all the work of Lexcen the genius. The New York Yacht Club sought to prove otherwise. One or two Dutchmen who had been involved when Lexcen, with the express permission of the New York Yacht Club, had tested his designs in Holland, claimed, somewhat excitedly, that they were the designers of the keel and not he. Yet when the NYYC sent emissaries to try to make the Dutch scientists sign affidavits to that effect, they could get no takers. The undercurrent of intrigue did not engender a friendly state of affairs between the Australians and the Americans and the mud-slinging continued until the very last minute. Even then it was a close call as to whether the NYYC would allow *Australia II* to race for the cup.

Australia II had posted the quality of her challenge all over Newport. A summer scoreline of forty-eight wins and six defeats from the selection trials was an adequate statement of the superiority of the challenger and it was this that led the Americans to fear, for the first time, that the cup might leave the hallowed portals of the NYYC in Manhattan after the longest winning streak in the history of international sport.

Lexcen had seen the critical path to success. Newport had never been a place of strong winds in September, which would point to the advantage of having a boat with the largest possible sail area. In

The slings and arrows of 'Keelgate' were almost terminal for Ben Lexcen. The designer who came under excessive fire from the New York Yacht Club, which accused him unfairly of not being the originator of the winged keel, suffered a minor heart attack prior to the cup races.

Left
There are times when almost everything goes wrong – and this was not *Defender*'s day. She chose to break her mast when *Sail* magazine editor Keith Taylor was on board.

the past, however, these 12-Metres had tended to be tender, falling over to large angles of heel in very little wind. The small boats had the advantage of being able to tack fast and accelerate quickly, and Lexcen found the way to combine the advantages and eliminate the one unattractive tendency. Even if the winged keel were not hydrodynamically better, it had the advantage of putting a great deal of lead in the wings, down low where it had the greatest statical leverage to keep the boat upright. It was noticeable in the summer of 1983 that whenever one went out into Newport Sound there were several pairs of Twelves duelling away in the haze. It was always easy to find *Australia II* – she was the more upright of one of those pairs: all the rest adopted much the same angle of heel.

With the design of *Australia II*, Lexcen also removed much of the lateral area underwater which made the boat 'turn on a dime'. It was this manoeuvrability which the Americans feared and which her opponents in the pre-starts of the selection trials were wont to avoid. Each one tried her out and were shocked to find just how quickly the Australian boat could turn, always inside her opponent, and just how soon they were up to speed and how much she had gained. Small wonder that the New York Yacht Club's hierarchy wanted to call off the cup races. It probably was not all to do with the boat, although to hear any of her opponents you would conclude that she was fearsome enough. The skipper and crew of *Australia II* were the best-trained and most experienced that that yachting country could offer and the entire squad was working together in a relentless steamroller-type operation fuelled by the knowledge that they had a real chance to pull it off.

If any writer had been commissioned by a film producer to write a scenario for an America's Cup film and had submitted what is now historical fact, he would have been despatched in short order, a hollow laugh ringing in his ear, having been told that what he suggested was simply not likely enough to

Flying Dutchman World Champion and Olympic silver medallist, Terry McLauglin, skippered *Canada 1*; an aggressive and thoroughly competitive skipper who seldom smiles.

Right above
Laser designer Bruce Kirby has long been a 12-Metre aficionado and was granted his first commission as a designer with *Canada 1*, a boat which showed great potential but which was woefully short of finance.

Right below
Australia II leading *Liberty*, a sight which became familiar to all those who watched the 1983 cup races both afloat and glued to television screens ashore.

be acceptable. After the shufflings of the early summer with boats not working or failing to come up to expectations, and the flurry of activity of the trials with some underdog supremacy (by *Courageous*), the totally unbelievable story of the cup races would have had any film producer angry at being expected to accept it. But it happened that way in real life. There was even a day's delay when the wind shifted around so much that the race committee was unable to set a course.

The first race was a shock. The challenger led at the weather mark! When *Liberty* surged into the lead on the second reach, the Americans breathed a sigh of relief, but *Australia II* came back and might have made the front again on the run had not her steering failed. It left *Liberty* to sail home to a seventy-second victory, but Conner must have understood what he was up against.

In the second race *Australia II* was hampered when her mainsail halyard car, which carries the mainsail headboard to the masthead, collapsed with six minutes to go to the start. The sail dropped approximately 18 inches, and to keep the leech tight for the beat, the crew of *Australia II* had to rake the mast forwards. Doing this destroys the upwind tune of the boat, yet even so *Australia II* was first to the weather mark by forty-five seconds. Her lead was narrowed on the two reaches; and on the second beat Conner made Bertrand tack out of phase with the wind shifts, and when *Australia II* sailed into a 'hole' *Liberty* went ahead and won the race by a minute and a half in a dying northerly breeze. There was even a protest for the Americans to answer and the meeting went on for much of the day, but the international jury ruled in favour of the defending country.

After that lay-day the real truth of *Australia II*'s ability began to emerge. On a light day she led by nearly six minutes at the last mark but the wind did not allow her to finish within the five-and-a-quarter-hour time limit. It was a race which John Bertrand was later to describe as 'the turning point',

Together here in 1974, when they were involved with Alan Bond's first challenge for the America's Cup: Hugh Treharne and John Bertrand. They were to be together again when *Australia II* won the cup, and then in the key roles of tactician and skipper.

Overleaf
Challenge 12 was Ben Lexcen's first design for 1983. She showed considerable promise in her early days against *Australia II* in Melbourne but in Newport sadly lacked new sails to make her competitive.

even if it had no effect on the scoreline. Conner, grateful for the reprieve, was heard to utter, 'God must be an American.'

The next day *Australia II* confirmed the world's suspicions in a 7-knot breeze. She won, going away, by three minutes and fourteen seconds – the biggest winning margin of a challenger ever. It was a short-lived record.

The fourth race demonstrated that Dennis Conner was the best 12-Metre match-racing sailor in the world. He had called for a lay-day in the hope of more wind, but God was perhaps not an American after all and there was only around 10 knots. Then Conner did what everyone expected him to do. He dominated the race. A well-chosen tack near the weather mark enabled *Liberty*, on port tack, to cross ahead of *Australia II* and from then on it was simply a matter of covering to stay ahead. Dennis is the master of that and the scoreline read 3–1.

The smiles were back on the faces of the Americans who drank that evening in the Candy Store. Conner and *Liberty* had only to win one more race for the cup to be safe. The odds were definitely in America's favour and the Mount Gay rum was doing its job.

The next day sobriety came fast. With less than an hour to go to the start, a small hydraulic ram at the end of *Liberty*'s port jumper strut burst. Without it there was no control of the top of the mast on port

tack. A radio call to the shore had a new part on its way out almost immediately, while Tom Rich and Scott Vogel went up the mast to clear the old one away. Theirs was the worst job of the cup summer: fifty minutes up the mast in 15–18 knots of breeze, bashed about by the motion of the boat in the sea chopped up by hundreds of spectator craft. Just how they affected the repair is their secret, but they did so with the ten-minute gun already fired as they came down the mast. However, they knew that the repair was unlikely to hold as the new ram was longer, by 2 inches, than the one it replaced.

Add to *Liberty*'s confusion the luff tape ripping off the genoa as it was hoisted, and the odds were very much on the Australians winning the race, but at the start John Bertrand committed what he called 'an error of truly grotesque proportions'. He was one second too soon across the starting line. After re-rounding the America's Cup buoy, *Australia II* was thirty-seven seconds behind *Liberty* – and this was the all-important race for *Australia II*, for if she lost, her cup challenge was over.

Four minutes into the race, the replacement hydraulic ram on *Liberty*'s port jumper strut gave way. Conner was ahead and gambled by going for the right-hand side of the course, knowing that to win the race he had to be in front at the first mark. The wind shift which he had hoped for never came and *Australia II* led by twenty-three seconds at the first mark and went on to win by one minute forty-seven seconds. The score was now 3–2.

Newport has its funny quirks just like any sailing venue, and during the first beat of the sixth race of the series it had one in full view of a large spectator fleet. God swapped sides. If he had been an American a few days earlier, he had decided that the balance should be applied and the Australians granted a favour. Conner had won the start and was covering *Australia II*. Bertrand put in a short hitch on starboard tack to clear his wind and then tacked back on to *Liberty*'s hip in a 15-knot nor'wester. Almost as soon as she tacked, Bertrand was able to

Alan Bond made four challenges before his aim was realised. He still maintains that his ultimate desire was to defend the America's Cup off Fremantle.

point *Australia II* 15–20 degrees closer to the mark than *Liberty* in a slightly fresher breeze. The wind had backed only for the Australians – *Liberty* did not get this shift for quite a while. It took *Australia II* to a two-and-a-half-minute lead at the weather mark and to a new record margin of victory for a challenger of three minutes and 25 seconds. With the score at 3–3 there was just one race to go to decide the winner of the America's Cup.

I remember working late that evening in the Armory, the Newport Press Centre, before going to The Ark for dinner with Australian radio commentator Stan Zemanek and his wife. We could not believe our luck: never in our lives had there been such a story. We were to watch the race of the century, only Alan Bond had decided that we should wait a day. He felt that *Australia II* needed a thorough check-out and the crew some relaxation after coming from 3–1 down to level the series.

The delay was to be even greater, however. Conner had used his multiple certificate to optimise *Liberty* for light-air sailing on the lay-day and it looked as though he had it right. Saturday 24 September was a day when the wind was so light and shifty that the race committee called it off. And then Dennis Conner requested a lay-day in the hope of stronger winds on the Monday. There were some tight-lipped faces in the bars of Newport throughout the weekend. At Cove Haven *Liberty*'s crew played the waiting game all Sunday – while Dennis Conner played golf – taking the mast out of the boat to check everything but leaving their ballast in the light-air mode.

They had chosen correctly. After one attempt at starting, the two boats went off an hour late into a light southerly breeze. *Australia II* led in the early stages of the first leg, but towards the top mark *Liberty* benefited from a header and Conner tacked on to port to clear *Australia II*'s bows and rounded the buoy twenty-nine seconds ahead. The horns blared and the sirens screamed; there was joy in America's heaven.

The afterguard of *Liberty*: Dennis Conner, at the wheel, has probably sailed more 12-Metre miles than any other America's Cup skipper; Halsey Herreshoff, the navigator, whose grandfather, Nathaniel, designed America's Cup defenders; and Tom Whidden, the sailmaker and tactician.

The heroes prior to the start of the fifth race, Tom Rich and Scott Vogel, who spent fifty minutes up the mast of *Liberty* repairing the port jumper strut.

Liberty held her lead, although it was cut to twenty-three seconds on the two reaches, and Conner sailed the leg of a lifetime on the second beat to be fifty-seven seconds ahead. It appeared that the cup would stay in America.

Both boats held a starboard tack until, somewhat inexplicably, *Liberty* gybed. Conner felt that the wind had shifted sufficiently for this to be a paying move. On *Australia II* Hugh Treharne, the tactician, called for Bertrand to hold a starboard tack. He had spotted a darkening of the water further out to the right. It could only mean one thing, an increase in the wind speed. As *Liberty* took the tactically correct tack to the leeward mark, *Australia II* made the strategic gain when she hit the slightly stronger wind. When the two boats closed three quarters of the way down the leg, they were level.

Conner then made an attempt to cover but Bertrand had a trick still up his sleeve. He sailed *Australia II* more downwind and when Conner tried to copy the manoeuvre he found that in that sailing angle *Australia II* had a noticeable advantage. It was

Never flustered, never ruffled even, Hugh Treharne was the ideal foil for John Bertrand. As tactician aboard *Australia II* Treharne called the shot which finally sealed the fate of the America's Cup.

there that the race was won, and lost. *Australia II* rounded the last mark with a twenty-one-second advantage and the battle for her to stay there began in earnest.

Bertrand knew that he had to stay between *Liberty* and the finishing line, no matter what Conner did. Conner tacked forty-seven times on that final leg and each time Bertrand covered his opponent. It was classic match-racing stuff. Conner was waiting for just one mistake by the Australians and they in their turn were careful not to make any. One could scarcely draw breath as the 'little white pointer' tacked each time in front of 'the red boat'. Slowly came the awareness that the cup was about to change hands, the awesome possibility that the men from down under were to plunder the silverware from the holy of holies.

Australia II crossed the finishing line forty-one seconds ahead; forty-one seconds that were to change the face of yachting history and, as when the brave Horatius swam the Tiber after holding the enemy at bay, 'even the ranks of Tuscany could scarce forbear to cheer'.

Bond's ambitions were almost complete. The bastion had been successfully stormed. Western Australia was on the map. The cup was going to have to be unbolted. The celebrations could begin and Newport's citizens would have to think of another way of life.

The images of the press conferences which followed are unforgettable. Conner, on the very edge of losing emotional control, was a dignified loser who congratulated Bond and said, 'Today, *Australia II* was just a better boat. And they beat us.' For a man whose autobiography is entitled *No Excuse to Lose*, Conner was true to the maxim and offered none.

The entire Australian team came into the Armory and were introduced by the syndicate manager, Warren Jones, the man to whom much of the credit for this win was due. He then likened the whole summer to a game of chess and said that on this day it was 'Mate'.

8 THE 1986 WORLD CHAMPIONSHIP

It was Alan Bond who went to some length to announce before the championship began that its result would have no bearing on the outcome of the America's Cup. He openly argued that match racing was so different from fleet racing that he would be surprised if the ultimate winner of the championship would be the correct vessel for the America's Cup, let alone a serious contender to win it the following year. At the end of the sixth race of the series, when the championship was decided with one race still to go, Australian yachting journalist Rob Mundle took great delight in asking Alan Bond if he still held those views after Colin Beashel had steered *Australia III* to victory. Just for once Bond was speechless – for a moment at least!

There can be no doubt that 12-Metre sailors enjoy fleet racing. That is the type of racing they know best in other classes and for which they get little opportunity in the Twelves. There came, early in 1986, a heaven-sent opportunity for them to indulge themselves. The World Championship came close to the end of the Fremantle summer, at the same time that the America's Cup would be held the following year – a chance to sample the conditions and to size up some of the opposition without too much at stake.

The temptation was sufficient to attract fourteen entries, the greatest number of 12-Metres racing together for close to half a century. Naturally it was spectacular and the racing was more open than many had predicted. And despite Alan Bond's prognostications, the World Championship provided an indication on the way that the class was developing. Above all, however, it was a 12-Metre fiesta.

There can be no better bench mark than the boat which previously won the Cup. *Australia III* tunes up for the World Championship against *Australia II*.

Sadly, one of the home teams elected not to compete. There had been a threat that the ruling of the International Yacht Racing Union to make 12-Metre racing certificates available after 'a yacht's first regatta' would release all the competing yachts' details immediately after the racing. It was more than enough to deter the Parry syndicate, even when the ruling was rescinded so that the certificates would not be released until just before the challenger and defender selection trials were held. The two Kookaburras therefore had their own series and all twenty-two of their crew members were disappointed. They too wanted to flex their muscles in the big league and perhaps take home the trophy. They kept their secrets, but at a price.

Fremantle in February is almost guaranteed to give more than adequate breeze for racing but as Carl Ryves, the tactician of *Australia III* so succinctly put it, 'As usual, it's not normally like this here.' The phrase is one known to every sailor who has left his home waters to attend a regatta. It was often true for this championship, although the Fremantle Doctor (a fickle surgeon in some eyes) was in evidence on occasion.

It brought home the fact that Fremantle and Newport were very different places and in two weeks there were more masts broken than in a couple of decades in Rhode Island Sound. For years 12-Metres had been set up for relatively light airs and long rolling seas; the fresh breezes and the short lumpy seas that the Indian Ocean produces over the reef crowned by Rottnest Island are very different. The effect of the seas is that they stop even 12-Metres almost dead in their tracks and the rigs, unaware of the effect of the waves, continue. The combination can be spectacularly disastrous.

As if to make his boss eat his words. Colin Beashel managed to co-ordinate the efforts of his crew and boat far better than he had been doing all summer and won the World Championship with one race still to be sailed. It might not have been a true measure of *Australia III*'s superiority: rather an indictment of

Above
The end of *New Zealand 5*'s chances of a Championship win. Chris Dickson was early across the starting line and had to go back.

Below
The jubilant crew of *French Kiss* after the first of their World Championship wins.

the competition. For a while it appeared it was possible for the Bond camp to provide not only the winner but also the runner-up, but in the later stages of the regatta the wind was fairly strong, conditions in which *Australia II* has always been vulnerable, and the 'one-two' was not to be.

The earliest of the major side issues of the championship concerned the name of one of the boats. When Serge Crasnianski decided to sponsor the challenge of the Société des Régates Rochelaise through his huge international company Kis and to name the first of the boats *French Kiss*, there were bound to be those who believed that International Yacht Racing Rule 26, concerning advertising on yachts, was being broken, among them the Royal Perth Yacht Club.

The club forbade Marc Pajot and his crew entry for the two practice races if they insisted on retaining the name *French Kiss*. They took the form of 'Invitation Races' and as such were not part of the championship proper and thus not under the direct jurisdiction of the International Yacht Racing Union; the club therefore could do as it sought fit. The boat took part in the first of these races, as an unofficial entry, and led until her mast went over the side. The French, seeing this as something of an omen, began negotiations to retain the name, but the organising club was adamant that in their opinon *French Kiss* contravened the rules. The French were not keen to change the name, which was to come under the review of an international jury immediately prior to the championship proper, but agreed to race under their sail number F7 only for the second practice race. Their decision was a wise one, satisfying as it did the Royal Perth Yacht Club, but leaving the way clear for the international jury to allow them to use the name *French Kiss*.

That decision, made by a jury composed of very senior International Yacht Racing Union judges, may prove to have greater effect than any other concerning the 12-Metres for many years. It showed how close the international jury would allow yachts'

names to relate to their commercial sponsors and prompted the speculation as to whether Alan Bond would dare to name the next boat for his syndicate *Fourex*, reflecting as it would the involvement of the Castlemaine Toohey breweries and their product XXXX. The French were jubilant.

A competitive gathering of fourteen boats one year prior to the America's Cup had never before happened in the history of the 12-Metre Class. There had not been that many competitive boats available before and this time the muscle flexing had some lightheartedness about it (if one was prepared to believe the syndicates' publicity), while the 12-Metre sailors were keen to grapple with each other on the water. The parallel arm wrestling championship for crews, held in the Auld Mug Tavern, had to be cancelled when one of the contestants broke an arm.

The 12-Metre aficionados, as well as the sailors, were in Fremantle to see this championship. It was a spectacle, quite unlike any previous 12-Metre regatta. It provided a real chance for those of us who have to write about the class, and to predict the outcome of the America's Cup, to assess the relative performances of the current crop of 12-Metres in a way that had been denied us in the past. The New York Yacht Club had always seen fit to keep the potential cup defenders well away from the opposition, but this time even the straw-hatted, red-trousered brigade approved of *America II* racing against fellow challengers and possible defenders. The old order had changed.

The championship revealed what Ben Lexcen had done to provide Alan Bond with a worthy successor to *Australia II*. The new boat was bigger than 'the little white pointer', but not by much. Benny's changes were subtle: a little more displacement on a slightly longer waterline length and a new winged keel which, though it was hidden from prying eyes by a modesty skirt when *Australia III* was hauled out of the water, was acknowledged to be different from the first 'three-dimensional' keel to hit the class. The

Above
The new *Azzurra* has not shown the same flair as her earlier sister for the Aga Khan headed syndicate.

Below
The sea is swept by the stern of *South Australia* as she bears off to return to the correct side of the starting line with five minutes to go to the fifth race of the World Championship.

124

wings were set further back and were slightly wider and thicker than her predecessor's.

What Ben Lexcen seemed to have aimed for was better performance in breezier conditions; *Australia II*, after all, was designed for relatively light-weather dominance. There is no doubt that Lexcen's calculations were correct as that is exactly how Colin Beashel was able to display the new boat. *Australia III* went well, both upwind and down, in the stronger breezes; when the wind was light, however, the new boat was not everything that Beashel would have liked. He had the experience of Carl Ryves, a well-rounded dinghy sailor, to call the shots for him; Grant Simmer, the navigator he had worked with during the 1983 campaign; and the brilliant artisanship of Damien Fewster as bowman. The hard core of experience was in the right places and Beashel produced the searing, in-bred talent which Bond had predicted just when it was most needed.

Bond's old boat was everybody's benchmark. How reassuring it must be for his syndicate's sailors that they had the boat which won the cup as a constant source of information. But how did skipper Gordon Lucas tackle the championship? He knew the limitations of *Australia II* better than his rivals, but they suspected the truth – the evidence of what went on between her and *Liberty* when the wind piped up on Newport has been well documented. When the wind did turn light, however, Lucas, with the ever-reliable Hugh Treharne as tactician, and two other of the cup-winning crew in 'Skip' Lissiman and 'Chink' Longley in the middle of the boat, proved that she was still the fastest 12-Metre in the world in those conditions. She also proved conclusively that she will not be the Cup boat a second time around. Fremantle is a place of brisk winds for the majority of the time and *Australia II* is no longer the right tool. Her pensioning pennant was soon to be brought out.

Had the first of her successors, *South Australia*, been well sailed, there is little doubt that she would

South Australia was the first of Ben Lexcen's designs to be built after *Australia II*. She has shown bursts of speed in all conditions but never any consistency.

Right
The poetry in motion that is a 12-Metre sailing to windward is amply displayed by *America II* (US 42), the first of the New York Yacht Club syndicate's three boats for 1987.

Left above
From left to right: *South Australia*, *Courageous IV*, *Italia* and *Azzurra II* beating to the finishing line in the final race of the World Championship.

Left below
New Zealand 5 doubled her sailing time during the first practice race and went on to win the first race of the 1986 World Championship – a remarkable achievement by a boat so new.

have been ahead. Lexcen designed the 'Croweater's' boat to be the first improvement on the cup winner, and with a new keel she sometimes displayed the correct amount of speed. It was, however, never sustained and her potential was rarely realised. The long period of assessment for *South Australia* came to an end with this championship. Her best place was a fourth, gained by going well to the left-hand side of the course on the first beat, in the same way as *Australia II* on the day she won in light airs. *South Australia* had been second and should have held her place, but she lacked the finesse in her afterguard – certainly there was no killer instinct.

The potential defenders of the America's Cup won four races between them. *Australia II's* victory was in the fourth race on a day when the start had been delayed for an hour to wait for the wind to fill in, a day very reminiscent of Newport. Gordon Lucas kept the light-displacement Twelve rolling all the way to the port tack lay-line – a long twenty-three-minute tack – and took advantage of a wind shift to leave the fleet trailing in his wake.

In the third race *Australia III* took the first of her wins in a building breeze, the race finishing in 20 knots. She came from behind in that one but led the fifth and sixth races for most of the time. Beashel has an old head on young shoulders and his undoubted talent contributed greatly to the success of *Australia III* in this championship, but so too did Ben Lexcen's design skill. The new boat did not, however, appear quite as happy in the lighter conditions and indeed, in their practice sessions, *Australia II* had almost always shown greater speed in winds of 10 knots and under. Vulnerability in light airs could be upsetting for a potential defender, or challenger, for the America's Cup with many of the early trial races held in the season before the Fremantle Doctor is on call.

French Kiss won two of the other races – the second and the last – and demonstrated that there are other paths to design success. Philippe Briand designed this boat without recourse to the testing tanks. He had, however, carried out considerable computer research and refined his design by the direct application of these studies. Marc Pajot and his crew, for all their relative inexperience in this class, showed that when the wind blowed fairly hard they were a force to be reckoned with, and that given better sails they might be very serious contenders for the America's Cup. By the end of the championship it was *French Kiss* that was on everyone's lips.

For sheer inexperience and the blissful ignorance of it, it was the Kiwis who took the biscuit. At the end of the first practice race they had doubled their sailing time with *New Zealand 5* during the day! On that day, however, the boat had led around the first triangle – first to the first mark in her first race. There was no doubting the 'plastic fantastics', as their syndicate head, Michael Fay, described the first two glassfibre 12-Metres in the world. They finally wound up in fourth and fifth positions in that race, but by the time the regatta began in earnest ten days later, Chris Dickson, the skipper of *New Zealand 5*,

Yves Pajot, Olympic silver medallist and skipper of the Marseilles syndicate. Pajot hopes to emulate his brother Marc and steer a challenger in 1987.

Left
The foredeck of *Victory '83* awash as she runs down-wind off Fremantle. Four men went into the sea because of waves sweeping them from the boats during this Championship.

Overleaf
Crewmen on *Courageous IV* prepare to drop the spinnaker as she approaches the leeward mark just outside *Challenge 12*.

had learned enough about his boat to take it to the front and keep it there.

The Kiwi attitude to sailboat racing applied to the 12-Metres does threaten to open a new dimension in the class. Dickson and Graeme Woodroffe, who skippered *New Zealand 3* (they use only odd numbers because Dickson does not favour even ones and Fay's lucky number is 7 – which will be on the stern of the 12-Metre the Kiwis will use for the America's Cup), have a string of international successes behind them. They clearly stated that they were treating the 12-Metre Class in exactly the same way as they would any other and that they were not overawed by the challenge they faced. They may well have discovered the correct attitude for tackling the very steep learning curve ahead of them: 12-Metre success generally comes as a result of progressive learning, and combining that with their natural talent could put them right at the forefront of the class. Dickson, with a consistent series, delighted his fellow countrymen – a sailing-mad nation if ever there was one – by taking second place in the championship.

The series alerted all the competitors to the hazards of racing 12-Metres in fresh winds and steep short seas. Broken masts, blown-out sails, men overboard and a boat close to sinking were all part of the rich pattern off Fremantle – each one a problem which the fourteen challengers and six defenders face in the long cup summer of 1986/7. Even the most experienced competitors, the Americans from the New York Yacht Club, fell foul of the elements and lost the championship because of mistakes or failures.

John Kolius of the USA had been sailing 12-Metres almost daily since 1982 when he was the skipper of *Courageous*. Yet even he could not maintain a trouble-free record. *America II* crossed the line first in each of the practice races, seemingly proving that experience had no peer in 12-Metre racing, and when she narrowed the gap between her and *New Zealand 5* on every leg of the course, it appeared

Chris Dickson, the youngest of 1987's crop of America's Cup helmsmen, has three times been the World Youth Champion.

Right above
New Zealand 5 and *Italia* manoeuvring close to the leeward mark.

Right below
Australia II was designed for conditions off Newport and while a good light-air bench mark for the Bond syndicate, cannot be seriously regarded as an America's Cup contender in the boisterous conditions generally found off Fremantle.

Start of the fifth race of the 1986 World Championship. Harold Cudmore bags the pin end with *Challenge 12* (F 5).

French Kiss, with considerable aft rake on her mast, performing well to windward in breezy conditions.

Left
Challenge 12 leads *True North* into the gybe in race five. The French-owned, Australian built and designed boat, which has been in Italian hands, was manned by a largely British crew led by Harold Cudmore in this regatta.

Overleaf
Crews prepare for action at the gybe mark.

that an American win was a certainty. But things began to go wrong for the Americans shortly after they had rounded the weather mark to begin the second run. As they gybed, the spinnaker wrapped itself around the forestay, and, since it was a much-loved sail, there was hesitancy in cutting it away and setting a replacement. Her crew struggled to free the 'chute as *America II* went from being in front to seventh place.

In the fifth race disaster again struck *America II*. She blew out a spinnaker on the first reach and then had a man overboard as she went into the leeward mark at the end of the second reach. That was caused by an unforgivable mistake. The bow man had gone out to the end of the spinnaker pole to trip the sail and the pole topping lift was not made fast. Just as soon as he tripped the snap shackle at the end of the guy, the outer pole end fell into the water taking him with it.

America II then lost the final race when her mainsail tore on the end of one of her jumper struts on the last run. Kolius had to nurse the sail all the way up the windward leg to the finish, and without full leech tension was unable to hold off the challenge of *French Kiss*. The additional points incurred for all those mistakes saw *America II* in third place rather than the top spot which should have been hers. She was the best all-round boat at the championship and had been set up for the series with one of her keels which had a wingspan of 3.8 metres – almost as wide as the vessel and the very limit of keel width in the class.

Beyond fifth place in the championship there was perhaps only one boat of real value, *True North*. This Steve Killing design for the Royal Nova Scotia Yacht Club showed that there was some potential in

The Giorgetti and Magrini designed *Italia* for the Yacht Club Italiano shows remarkable similarity to the Ian Howlett designed *Victory '83* now also owned by that syndicate.

Fourteen 12-Metres head for the second mark – a rare sight in yachting.

her in the stronger breezes; her worst race was the fourth when the wind was light. The Italians, for all their promise in the past, had nothing to show for their pains except a guaranteed return to the drawing board in an effort to justify their high-profile presence in Fremantle, a town of considerable Italianate background, for the following cup summer. *Courageous*, sporting the suffix '*IV*' to denote another new vortex-winged keel, was almost the oldest 12-Metre present, and even the influx of new blood into her crew could not push her as fast as the newer boats, a state of affairs which Gordon Ingate and his crew on *Gretel II* were also able to appreciate – the 1970 challenger's highest moment coming when she placed seventh in the second practice race due to five disqualifications and two retirements.

Pushing an old boat around the course gave Harold Cudmore and some members of the Royal Thames Yacht Club's challenge the opportunity to view their future opposition at first hand. Cudmore has the philosophy that it is better to sail in any regatta than to miss it, and the generosity of Chris Griffiths is providing *Challenge 12* for him to sail when the Marseilles syndicate had returned to France for fund raising gave the nominated British skipper an additional chance to exercise his talents in the arena. Poor sails and a tired boat did not give him much opportunity to shine, but he definitely worried some in the fifth race when he had the best start and went the right way up the first leg. The nadir came on the final day when a pump hose accidentally came off and the boat was very close to sinking, needing help from HMAS *Geraldton* in the form of a diesel pump to maintain her in the floating mode.

9 LOOKING FORWARD TO 1987

When in 1983 Robert Stone, the commodore of the New York Yacht Club, handed over the America's Cup to Peter Dalziel, his counterpart from the Royal Perth Yacht Club, he began a new era. At the Marble House, a former Vanderbilt mansion, Alan Bond was given the bolt which had held the cup to its plinth and Ben Lexcen was presented with a flattened automobile hubcap to commemorate what he had threatened to do if *Australia II* had won the cup, thereby converting it into the 'Australian Plate'. It was a moment of humour as well as of history in a township which had seen so much of cup racing and was about to see its departure.

Earlier that day I had written of Newport, the home of the 12-Metres, for *The Guardian* under the heading 'Requiem for a racing town'. It summed up my feelings for a place I too loved and which had been so much a part of my image of 12-Metres.

"Newport, Rhode Island, is fiercely proud of its heritage. Like the New Englanders themselves, the town is steeped in early colonial history and it was, until yesterday, the home of America's Cup races. Huge billboards on the side of the highways proclaim that fact as you enter Rhode Island – 'the greatest little state in the Union'; 'the Ocean State'. Now they will have to go and Newport is bereft of its jewel.

"Despite the parties following the presentation of the cup, Newport itself was stilled in the early hours. Even the clapboard houses seemed to have withdrawn: up Pelham Street, the first in America to have been lit by gas – by David Melville in 1805 – to the intersection; along Spring Street past the spotlit white-wooded spire of Trinity Church to the imposing pillared facade of the Littlefield-Van Zandt

Harold Cudmore, skipper of the 1987 British challenge, a specialist in match racing, won the Congressional Cup, the second most important match-racing event in the world, in the year immediately prior to his challenge.

Left
The Americans and Italians get together in their early training, a hitherto unthought-of co-operation, but it is the America's Cup which is the prize and the Australians the common enemy.

145

The America's Cup buoy, seven miles off Newport, a mark which may never again be layed. This buoy was only placed in position by the US Coastguards in America's Cup summers.

House. In the tiny cemetery next door a squirrel busied himself burying hazelnuts, blissfully unaware that a few hours earlier Newport real estate values had taken a severe knock. Without the cup many of the large houses will never again find a full summer's rent – between them the ten syndicates this summer rented more than twenty of varying sizes.

"I walked past the Capitol Realty Company, to which I had given money in 1974 while Alan Bond, Ben Lexcen and John Bertrand – this year's triumphal trio from Western Australia – put together their first effort with a boat called *Southern Cross*, a bright-yellow 12-Metre known familiarly as 'the Custard Bucket.' The Realty Company will not see my pennies again or those of a good many higher rollers besides.

"What will become of the bars, bistros and boutiques which, since the US fleet left town in 1970, have sprung up on the wharves? Can Newport without the cup support their vast numbers? Mere tourists will not seem so attractive as the 12-Metre

sailors who are reputed, by their presence in Newport for the racing, to help swell the annual turnover in Rhode Island State by $300 million. The Candy Store and the Black Pearl are institutions on Bannister's Wharf that will surely never perish. When Ted Turner won the cup in 1977 his crew were awarded gold cards – free drinks for life – at the Candy Store. Now perhaps they would be better off with similar facilities at the Tum Tum Tree in Fremantle.

"Newport will sleep uneasily this winter. No longer is it a dream world."

Fremantle has accepted the role of home base for the 12-Metres, but who knows for how long? The boats develop. There is a new style of 12-Metre being produced to deal with the more boisterous conditions that Fremantle waters regularly offer. The images change, but they are unblurred. 12-Metres are, like narcotics, addictive; like fine wine, con-

Above
The long days of 12-Metre racing begin and end with a tow out to the course. Off Western Australia this is as wet as any of the sailing.

Right
Kookaburra, a potential defender for Australia.